"HO...
SN...
WIZARD...
"COME KILL—IF YOU CAN!"

"Taratan, you traitor!" cried Princess Cyenia. "You were our man! May you plow the dry plains of Hither Hell forever!"

The crowd rumbled: "Taratan...Taratan..."

"This is foolish!" Taratan jumped on the dry fountain in the center of the square. "This is no way to choose the next king! It's stupid. Stupid! You can do better than this. Draw lots. Toss a coin. Play mumblety-peg! Any way would beat killing each other!"

"Wot's 'e on about?"

"Bloke's gone clean daft."

Princess Gaya was dark-faced with rage, Princess Cyenia laughed bitterly, Mohendro Sat roared with laughter.

"Get Taratan," someone said; and the mob, half ugly men, half demons, contested for the pleasure of destroying him.

"It's not enough," Taratan cried, hacking a lizard-headed man, "that I have to kill!" He kicked and dislodged a death grip on his ankle. "It's not enough that I have to—" pause for two strokes and a death scream—"have to mischoose kings!" Taratan's sword was red; it rained blood...

"But I have to do it for a shekel a day!"

→ → →

ROUNDED
WITH SLEEP

Also by Rob Chilson

Men Like Rats

Published by
POPULAR LIBRARY

ROUNDED WITH SLEEP

ROB CHILSON

POPULAR LIBRARY

An Imprint of Warner Books, Inc.

A Warner Communications Company

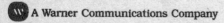

DEDICATED
to me.
—to the young boy who eagerly read *Conan*,
from the old man who wryly remembers.

Table of Contents

1

A Hero's Life

They had brought the Lion of Amara to bay.

Riandar stood with his back against a buttress of the Temple of Lel Makh. Before him lay a pile of dead and dying. Beyond them were others of their ilk: minions of Lord Vakhon. The lord sat his slender horse behind them, sharp-bearded hawk face expressionless. Behind Riandar on the thick buttress was the Slave Priestess, Trina, wearing nothing but the scanty sacrificial harness they had arrayed her in before he stole her from the Crypts of Doom in Scensifer, three days' ride to the north.

Above them all the priests of Lel Makh looked dispassionately down. Riandar's sacrilege in invading the Crypts, slaying the Great Serpent, and stealing the girl meant little to the priests of Lel Makh, devotees of a rival cult.

In the heat of the day's flight, Riandar had discarded his mail shirt, and had now thrown aside his tunic. He stood naked from the waist up, his mighty chest and brawny arms crossed with old scars and scabs, here and there bleeding lightly.

"Come on before night overtakes you!" cried Riandar, the Lion. "You have not your mothers to comfort you when it grows dark!"

The sunset hung bloody banners over the bloody field.

The lord's bravos formed a line. Riandar fell silent, eyes slitted, holding his long two-handed sword easily, red mane tossed back. At a cry from Lord Vakhon they came on at a trot, but broke to go around the pile of dead and wounded.

With a blurring speed that would have shamed the lion his namesake, Riandar bounded toward the right end of the line, swinging his great sword like a whirlwind. Longer than theirs, it held them off and for seconds he beat down their swords and made their caps ring. Dismayed, one killed by a crushing blow, they fell back.

Instantly Riandar plunged to his left to meet those who'd come around the other side of the pile. For long moments they resisted. At length they faltered. Again with that blurring speed he whirled toward the right end of the line, now formed up again and coming on, rather hesitantly.

Try as he might, Riandar could not overbear them. Trina gave a low cry of dismay. A fresh man, who had leaped atop the pile of bodies, sprang down at him.

With a disengage leap, Riandar sprang back to the buttress.

Confidently now the bravos came on. For the first time Lord Vakhon raised his voice, addressing Trina. "Fear not, little one, you shall be well cared for when your abductor's serving his apprenticeship in Hell."

Nothing could have been calculated to drive the Lion of Amara's bursting heart and limbs to greater exertion, though he had not breath to answer. Trina cried out and scrambled away when one of them sprang atop the buttress and came walking up to get behind him.

Riandar's breath came in gasps and perspiration streamed off him; his throat was rasped with each breath. Even his giant strength could not sustain him much longer. His blood-clotted red mane flew as he swung his great sword.

Just as the bravo behind him prepared to drop on his shoulders, the Lion of Amara pounced with the last hoarded drachm of his strength, shearing the head off one man. He beat down two swords and sent another man sprawling with his head ringing.

Riandar, gasping, had them hampered against the wall. Trina cried out in hope and fear. But three days of fighting and riding had taken their toll, and there'd been little sleep during the nights with Trina. Still the Lion of Amara fought on.

Riandar never felt the stroke that hamstrung him. He knew only that his swing went wide, that he was falling, that his sword had been struck aside by one of the bravos' shorter ones. The jackals closed in on the Lion. A cruelly grinning face flashed before him, straggly black beard, crooked teeth, broken nose; there was a gleam of steel, and a distant blow on his chest. He felt no pain.

Riandar was on his back on the sward, still gasping for breath and feeling now a bubbling in his chest. The battle was somehow very far away and unimportant. His eyes fell inconsequently on Trina, crouching agonized on the buttress and staring down, her peach-soft cheeks wet with tears .... Then the circle of steel-handed men closed and the bloody sky faded to black, to the sounds of thuds and grunts and the feel of being jolted. As the Lion of Amara rushed down into that dark sky, he was aware chiefly of regret that he had not had time for a final sup of wine. His throat was abominably dry...

He awoke in velvety, dim-red darkness, heart beating furiously, gasping for breath, making convulsive movements to rise and fall on again. But he was already on his feet, though not standing. He leaned against a slanting mattress.

Decanted again, he thought, observing the sourceless red light. He cleared his throat; the dryness was gone, but not the thirst. All exhaustion and wounds were washed away; he felt like a prime athlete in the pink of condition, as of course he was. But the death of the Lion of Amara was all too real, painless though it had been. He reclined in silence for some time, casting off those wrenching emotions. They were not, after all, strictly his; Riandar was a computer program.

Waking was like waking from a long, colorful, intense dream of being someone else. Riandar faded slowly from his mind, all his passions fading, from scarlet to pink, and the real essential self emerged. He felt that he was putting that self back together, fitting himself into life again. Reactivating all the personality programs in his sleeping brain, far from here. At last he was himself again.

Blown out of the Game.

I lost, he thought. Cut down, after twenty years with Riandar. But what mattered was how well he had fought; anybody could be outnumbered and overwhelmed.

At length he chuckled faintly as he dismissed his/ Riandar's agony for Trina, and slid his hand down the side of the slantboard. Light came slowly as he slid the switch. His eyes adjusted. He was in a very small room, a mere coffin, containing the slantboard and himself. He opened the door and stepped out into a gleaming white/ chrome resurrection room full of white-clad robots, medical equipment, a dozen other mirrored doors like his, and people, all as naked as himself.

This new body worked perfectly, of course, but though not surprised, he could not contain a feeling of delight at the precision of movement, the high good health, he felt. He felt like leaping and running. He turned to study himself in the mirror on the outside of the door.

He was a hero. The body had felt big; now he saw that his height was well over two meters, perhaps by as much as ten centimeters. The shoulders were broad even for that height, the arms as long and powerful as an ordinary man's legs. His hands were horn-hard and looked as if they could crush rocks, and the feet were horny-soled also. Even the penis was heroic.

He was brunet with steel-gray eyes, the black hair wavy and moderately long in back, bald-chinned and never needing to shave. The swarthy, sunburned body was crisscrossed with thin old scars denoting years of battle, and its synapses had been trained for all forms of combat.

Well, he thought, I earned it. I died a hero.

This was quite the most formidable hero he had ever been. He wondered who it was.

"Sir?" A robo doctor addressed him. It was a human body, with a very bland face, identical to all other robo doctors. Like his own, the body was synthetic, but it was animated by a computer, not a man. "May I help you?"

"No, thank you."

Brushing by it, he threaded through the equipment and robots toward a group of decantees who had gathered in a small lounge at one end of the resurrection room. He passed a brawny man sitting at a desklike instrument, talking to a robo doctor. ". . . left-handed," this one was saying, "always been left-handed. I don't think—"

"Oh, here's a hero!" cried a beautiful woman as he stepped into the lounge area. The lounge was a subtle sunset color, a pale sparkling wine with darker, straw-colored seats and a small table in a still darker tan. "Who are you?"

"Andy K. Thatcher."

A murmur of recognition went through them and he

flushed pleasantly. "I was lately Riandar, the Lion of Amara," he added unnecessarily.

"Oh, so he's dead. That'll alter a lot of things." For a few minutes they discussed the concomitant changes in the Game, the advance of Lord Vakhon chief among them.

"How did Riandar die?" a handsome woman asked.

Thatcher described his death briefly.

"No wonder you were promoted!" the woman said. "I don't suppose you remember me, but we played together a time or two. I'm Judy Somerset."

The name rang no bells. Thatcher looked her over, letting his pleasure show, and she smiled. She was tall and exceptionally well formed, with an imperial air and magnificent pointed breasts that needed no support, despite the apparent age of her body—late thirties.

"I suppose you're a queen, or princess. Or maybe a high priestess."

"I represent Authority, with this body," she said, looking down at herself in delight. "I just took delivery on it. I'll be a nobleman's wife, and run the duchy. I was Alula the serving wench at the Palace of Aksarben when you were the young hero—what was the name—"

"Akanax."

"Yes! I carried you a message one night, and you felt me up, but we never got it on, because you had to go kill someone."

"Does a nobleman's wife get much?" Thatcher asked. "I hoped you won't be bored."

"I'll have a lover among the serving lads," she said. "Actually, I had a choice of a sexy role or something quieter, and took the quieter one. I got too much last time—raped fourteen times while being beaten—fourteen times that I counted before I passed out. A meddling, sexy, nobleman's daughter, just asking for it," she added. "I was given to my father's enemy's henchmen."

"Hey, Thatcher!"

He turned to face a barrel-shaped fellow. This individual was gorilla built, with big chest, long arms, bandy legs, and a good-natured monkey face. Despite his belly and bowlegs, he looked competent and tough. A hero's sidekick and drinking companion.

"Hymie Siebert," he said. "But you don't remember me, Thatcher—likely you wouldn't even if I had my last face. I never thought the boys'd get you!"

"Oh, you were one of Lord Vakhon's bravos?"

"Right, promoted on account of the way I stood up to you, I guess. I got it three times—arm, neck, and I think head. Hey, guess what we have. C'mere, Aura."

A very young beautiful girl, middle or late teens, with a tempting lush body, who looked at him with wide eyes and moist lips.

Judy Somerset laughed. "A genuine virgin!" she said.

"No! It's been a lifetime or two since I saw one in the Game."

The girl nodded, looking at him eagerly. "I've been sacrificed five times as priestesses, and once I was killed to keep me from being raped." She tugged at his penis, eyes glowing. "Maybe *this* time I'll get it!"

"Good luck," said Thatcher, laughing and freeing himself. "But it probably won't be me. We heroes are a chivalrous lot."

A number of other decantees had joined them, including the left-handed complainer, and now there was a general cry of, "Oh, another hero!"

Thatcher and Aura turned to see a broad-shouldered, good-looking young man joining them. "Probably your man, Hymie," Thatcher said. "I usually play loners."

The young fellow had obviously just been promoted to hero. He looked around wide-eyed at the women. "I'm Adrian Rauh. I was Sindonian Chief Forester, and fought the Black Fox. Pretty well, evidently," he said, looking down at himself in shy delight. Then, gleefully, "Are you all slave girls?"

Laughing, the women surged around him, led by Aura, and Hymie followed to introduce them. Adrian gathered up a double armful and kissed them indiscriminately.

Thatcher felt a warm pressure on his bare left side as he stood laughing at the spectacle and remembering his own first hero role. Judy Somerset pressed magnificently against him.

"It'll be at least a week before you're wanted in the Game again," she said. "I'm scheduled for a month out of the Game myself. I don't know what your plans are, but I won't have much catching up to do, myself."

"Most of my friends are in the Game, since this is an unscheduled out. I do need to get back to Tangier and touch base," he said. "Unless this is Tangier."

They looked around, attracted the attention of a robot.

"This is the city of Kidal in the central Sahara—the middle of the great forest, near the Kingdom of Sindon and about ten days' ride from Scensifer. Tube connections to Tangier are available; it's about an hour's trip."

Judy lifted eyebrows at him.

Thatcher nodded. "I'll go to Tangier, then; see you there?"

"Yes, or you could follow me to Atlantis. I like beaches and swimming, and of course—"

All Africa was used in the Game, and the beaches were unavailable. "Why not?" he asked. "I'll be along in a couple of days."

Making their farewells to the group, they strolled out arm in arm and still quite nude, into the cool quiet corridors of the underground city of Kidal. A short walk through a high-vaulted, oyster-blue street brought them to a much wider and higher street that echoed faintly the whisper of the moving way in its middle. It took them quickly to the tube station, where they parted, Judy taking the tube to Dakar in the west.

Like the corridors and streets of all the underground cities of the Gamers' Age, the tube station was high and cool and quiet, its architecture austere, almost sparse, despite the marble columns and the ornate bronze gates. It was nearly empty; Kidal was a city primarily of robots. Fifteen minutes later, during which time Thatcher discovered that the tube station was a bit chilly for nudity, he slid gratefully into a car for Tangier. The car was slender, elegant, the last word in space-age design. Not streamlined, of course; the tube was evacuated. It floated above the tube channel, and Thatcher remembered that they had torn out all the magnetic levitation coils and replaced them with gravitic repulsion.

The car was but half occupied. He was ignored, and spent the hour to Tangier in solitary reflection.

Thatcher hadn't been alone now for many days, not merely in company with such as Trina and the riding companions of the adventure (abandoned in Scensifer), but thinking the violent thoughts and living the violent life of Riandar, the Lion of Amara. Now, for a few rare days—Thatcher was a dedicated Gamer—he was himself again, Andy K. Thatcher, in a new body. He promised himself a couple of days to catch his breath before going on to Atlantis.

Tangier. Tangier Underground, it had been called at first, until the old Tangier had been dismantled, its monuments carried below and solemnly set up again. He might still have been in Kidal; the city had the same cool spare design, the same economy of effect, the same timeless peace hanging under its high ceilings. City of the new age.

In the tube station, he was approached by a young-seeming woman who introduced herself and asked for the favor of his acquaintance. Not only was his hugely heroic body itself an attraction, but it was a symbol of status— the mark of immense success in the Game. Still seeking solitude, however, Thatcher begged off politely. A shy man, the approach made him nervous. Judy Somerset's approach had been all he could handle.

The direct route to his apartment was blocked off; they were extending the city tubeway. Thatcher hesitated, then what felt like memory came to him. In the vaults below Tangier, his sleeping original body was connected to this walking one by a radio link. The android body had no brain, merely a radio organ in the skull. The link was through a computer, which now inserted the knowledge of the shortest route.

After a further traverse of the sliding streets and corridors of the underground city, Thatcher found himself at the ornately-carved wooden door of his small apartment. With some relief he thumbed the recognition lock and slipped inside, stood looking around. It was four months since he'd been here. A century ago he had taken the best apartment he could afford. There was a vast master bedroom, which he used only when hosting parties, a small bedroom, a large and well-equipped exercise room, a sybaritic bathroom, the living room.

His furnishings were a contrast to the cool perfection of the rooms. There was a lion-skin rug on the master bedroom floor. He had killed the (computer-animated) thing when he was Rollory. Riandar had brought down that ibex with a javelin cast; a lucky shot. The vase, with its dried frond arrangement, was a bold, barbaric pottery wine jar from Ophir. The intricately-worked leather hanging was done by a caravan guard from the Zhemrian Empire, an old friend of Akanax's.

There was no hobby room; the living room had a video receiver and a bank of records. He subscribed to all the Games, of course. He did, however, read, and the bank contained books in text as well as video records. On a shelf were a few bound books, now a century old, mostly classics: Robert E. Howard, J. R. R. Tolkien, P. C. Hodgell, Fritz Leiber.

Thatcher walked through the apartment, finding all in order and unobtrusively clean. The window was transmitting a picture from the Eye of Balamok, the great statue in the city of Caramanx. The Mediterranean, impossibly blue and serene, with the sail of some adventuring galley going out: the Game went on.

Donning a too-small silk robe from his closet, Thatcher went to the bar and poured himself an abstemious small glass of wine from a hand-blown bottle: product of Gronderthal in what was once Germany. Farewell, Riandar; farewell, Lion. He drank. Then, with a humorous grimace, he washed the glass and set it aside. There was a cabinet of similar glasses in the living room; a trophy case. Each glass had the name of some adventurer or hero character, and a pair of dates; his career etched in glass.

Pouring a diet soda over ice, Thatcher stalked back to the front room and keyed the visiphone on. Its surface lit with a Roy G. Krenkel line drawing from a Tarzan book.

"Sword and Sorcery Game Central," said a robotic voice.

"Andy K. Thatcher," he said. "When will I be wanted in the Game again?—don't tell me my character's name."

"Not for at least two weeks. If you wish we could readily extend that another week."

"Thank you." He sipped. "What happened in Scensifer after Riandar died at the Temple of Lel Makh?"

The robot started to tell him, consulting both its memory of things past and its knowledge of the Script.

"Okay, that's enough; I don't want to know too much about the future." The script had variants that allowed for Riandar's death, his survival, his being besieged in the Temple under sanctuary, and so on. "Generally, how's the Game going? I don't know anything except the affairs of Scensifer and the nearby kingdoms for the past four months."

Central tersely briefed him on the international affairs of the Game and on the adventures of other notable figures in it. Thatcher made notes of particular episodes he wanted to view.

"Okay, thanks. Now, can you tell me what's going on in the world? How about the High Fantasy Game? Did the Elves make alliance?"

They hadn't, but the beleaguered humans had made a provisional alliance with the Dwarves. Thatcher nodded eagerly, making further notes. Sharp little war shaping up there; the High Fantasy Game was bigger even than S&S. It occupied all Eurasia. He went on with less interest to listen to the affairs of the Wild West Game in North America. The Seafaring Game was piddly stuff, mostly in Oceania; pirates and the like. Latin America and the Caribbean was given over to Romance, with Graustark contending against the Norstro-Huguenot Empire.

Of least interest to him, but for one item, was the Space Game. It tended to break up into various units because of light-speed lag. A body on the Moon, for instance, couldn't be animated from Earth, for the signal to move wouldn't be received by the body for a second and a half, and it would take another second and a half for the feedback to return.

Of course the bodies of the Gamers could all be on the Moon—but not if the adventure went off to Mars or the Asteroids. It meant that when the adventure ships went out, they had to have sealed compartments full of sleeping bodies and robots to tend them, which could make it hard on the programmed personalities of the animated bodies. They could be made to overlook much, but not all.

"What's the stage of terraformation of Luna?" Thatcher asked.

"Approximately a third complete as regards atmosphere and hydrosphere." said the computer. "Well over half complete as regards time to completion."

"Good."

Thatcher was intrigued with low gravity, though he had no interest in the rather moronic Space Game. When the terraformation of the Moon was complete, the Space Game would move away. Luna would be turned into a fairy land or maybe a Sword & Sorcery distant planet site. Thatcher was seriously considering putting in for that.

It was a foregone conclusion that when the Space Gamers finished terraforming Mars it' would be turned over to the Burroughs Bibliophiles. But that would not be for a half a century after Luna was ready to use.

A thought from his musings about the Space Game recurred to him. Impulsively—for the first time in fifty years—Thatcher asked, "Central, where's my body?"

It could be anywhere on Earth, of course.

"In the vaults under Tangier, sir."

Where he had left it. Thatcher nodded. He had only a vague awareness of what went into the answering of the question: it wasn't a thing that S&S Game Central would know about. Central had called up and asked whatever computer was in charge. In fact half a dozen computers, each smarter than Thatcher, might have cooperated to answer him, rather than inconvenience him by making him call the proper computer.

"Do you wish a readout check on its condition?"

"Oh, no. Just—it's okay?"

"Yes, it's in excellent condition."

"That's fine, then."

Thatcher felt uncomfortable. He sat here, nearly seven old English feet tall, the reward of innumerable successful battles and intrigues, a warrior, a victor, a man of consequence. The sleeping body was that of a slight, stooped dreamer who read books—lifetimes ago, when the Games were just beginning. It was embarrassing to be reminded of what he had been—to be reminded that he was linked by a slender radio umbilical to—that.

"Central, out. Phone, what messages have been received?"

The Krenkel illo disappeared and a list of names of friends who had left messages slid up the surface in chron order. The phone computer had thoughtfully starred those who were back in the Game, and Thatcher called a couple who were not, leaving messages. They were out, one in Antarctica.

He started to listen to the messages from the starred

names, then hesitated. He didn't feel like it. Tomorrow would be time enough. Thatcher stood up and paced around the room, went restlessly into the exercise room and worked desultorily on several of the machines.

It would be up to him now to keep this body in shape, but at the moment it needed no work. His chief memory of his first hero's role was of aching all the time, due to improper exercise.

He went back to the front room, keyed up an important episode from the Game, and went to get more soda. The episode was vividly recorded in color holo from thousands of hidden cameras and from the visual signals from animated bodies. In the Games, even most of the animals in the streets were animated, so the viewpoint was omnipresent.

He didn't care.

Thatcher turned it off, stood up, gulped at his soda, and felt a trickle of panic. There was the impulse to drink something far stronger. It would do no harm, of course. But the Game was so engrossing, so colorful and lifeful, that drink and drugs had little appeal to the Gamers.

Maybe he should call a doctor.

At this point he belatedly realized his problem. A doctor would tell him he was suffering from disengagement disorientation and might well prescribe a sedative. For a moment he wondered—he usually didn't think about such things—whether that would be administered to him or to his sleeping body. Maybe the animated body would be given a placebo.

A drink would do no harm in any case. Thatcher

reached for the gin, back at the back part of the bar he rarely touched.

Having drunk, he went to the small bedroom and immediately discovered that the little iron-framed bed was too small for his giant skeleton. The air bed in the master bedroom was too comfortable—it was like floating— but it would have to do. Adjusting the lights and starting music, he lay down and let his mind roam back over the career of Riandar, the Lion of Amara.

As conceived by the Writers, the Lion of Amara had entered the Game in his early twenties. That had been twenty years ago, and he had died somewhere in his early thirties. He was a member of a small tribe of fierce barbarians in the Mountains of the Moon—a name retained from the old Africa.

So. Twenty years ago Thatcher had awakened in the Lion's camp near Hangaman, had been Riandar—young, impetuous, bold, proud. He had ridden into Hangaman, gotten into a fight with caravan guards at the crude inn, been accepted as a guard to a rival caravan, and the adventure that was his life had begun.

The pace had been headlong for twenty years, during which time Thatcher had had only twenty-five respites— times during which Riandar had been out of the Game's story. After each time, when he had reawakened as Riandar, the computer had a detailed memory of the missing weeks and he had carried on as if no time had lapsed. For the composite mind that was Riandar, none had.

Riandar was not wholly a creation of the Writers, or of the computers which projected the constructed personality into the signal loop. Thatcher himself added an indefinable note to the whole, totally submerged though his own personality seemed to be while playing his role. That was why he was a great hero. After all, heroes started with equally good young hero bodies, and the roles were much alike. But he was something special . . . .

So thinking, he drifted off to sleep, his mind filled with images of flaming sunsets and the sound of thundering hooves, of scantily clad women, defiant/compliant, and the grunting exertions of battle, of blood, the dull ring of metal on metal and a distant chorus of male voices. . . .

2

The Lion of Atlantis

Thatcher needed a wardrobe to fit his new giant frame. But before going out, he spent a couple of days catching up, sending messages to absent friends, and just breathing. Being Andy K. Thatcher.

Buying clothes brought up the subject of money, and Thatcher approached his phone with trepidation.

"Finance Central." Picture of Scrooge McDuck's money bin.

"Uh—I was calling the Tangier branch of the Mendicants' Bank—"

"Your bank has been merged into the Central system, Mr. Thatcher. How may we help you?"

He supposed that was all right. They took pretty good care of things these days. "How am I doing? Am I in debt or anything?"

"No, sir, the Gameplayers' Trust paid off your debts fifty years ago."

"Good. Uh—how well off am I?"

"I do not understand the question."

"Can I afford—well, can I afford a trip to Atlantis?"

"Transportation is free, sir."

Thatcher paused to consider that. He distinctly remembered that as usual he had proffered his thumb to the eye of the tube system at Kidal. Was it no longer connected to the banking system?

"How about hotel space in Atlantis?"

"Housing is also free, sir."

"You mean—" He stared at the money bin. "I'm not paying anything for this apartment?"

"It was found, sir, that in an advanced robotic economy with unlimited sources of energy, money was an impediment to business. It was got rid of. Housing, food, clothing, transportation, and other items were produced so cheaply it did not pay to maintain the elaborate accounting systems money required."

Thatcher knew little about economics, and sat dumbfounded. "Uh—what about scarce natural resources?" he finally asked.

"Natural resources are not scarce in space, and the Space Game supplies vastly more than the human race can absorb."

"Then I can buy a new wardrobe."

"Yes, sir."

Thatcher sat in silence for some time, absorbing this. For many years he had assumed that, despite his success in the Game, he was on the verge of penury. He looked around the little apartment. Neat, cozy, very pleasant in fact. But—

"Could I have a better apartment?"

"Of course. You do understand, Mr. Thatcher, that we cannot give everyone the best. Thus, for every advance above a certain basic level, we must assign space by rank in society. Successful Game players such as yourself do not fare badly in these rankings, though productive workers such as technicians do better."

Thatcher nodded. The minority who worked had long gotten the best, though before this it was paid out in money. "Well, then, let me know what is available to me and I will think it over."

In truth he was not eager to move, now that he thought of it. This little apartment had been home for longer than people used to live, though he had spent an aggregate of, he supposed, not more than a couple of years in it in the century he had lived here.

Thatcher did not call Judy Somerset. Instead he consulted her public schedule, which told him she would be at a certain public party in Atlantis. He arrived at that party wearing a full formal tuxedo in pearl gray, which with his immense bulk and ultrapolite expression attracted all eyes.

The party was in one of the largest public halls of Poseidonis, the chief city of Atlantis. The hall—a series of grand rooms under barrel vaults, separated by colonnades— was far more ornate than most public buildings of the Gamers' Age. With its gilding and inlay work, it looked, in fact, like a rather subdued, but huge, throne room for a Game Kingdom.

A gushy hostess clad chiefly in lace approached him, asked his name, and repeated it in awe.

"Is Judy Somerset here yet?" he asked modestly.

A wave of murmur followed by a wave of silence preceded them through the throng; they knew his name. Judy was wearing a crinoline and hoops, the décolletage of which made the most of her remarkable physique. She looked at him in rapture, and it occurred to him for the first time that she had never believed he'd come. Uncomfortably he bent, that she might give his cheek the kiss of welcome.

"Good to see you, Andy," she said breathlessly. "These are my friends—" She introduced several women and a couple of men. All seemed awed to meet him and he was glad when she led him away toward the dance in the next room of the colonnaded hall.

"I hadn't realized that I was so notorious," he said, whirling her around.

"Oh, you're quite famous! One of the top heroes in all the Games."

"Hard to believe, by anyone who knows me well," he said. He danced perfectly, now that he had had time to reprogram his motions to fit his size. The computer in the link between him and his sleeping body not only stored phone numbers and faces, it also supplied the proper steps for any dance.

"Oh, you're as famous as Walter Hauk, Carol Wagner, or Francis Tumbo-Masabo, or even Ron Richter. Don't you follow the Games?"

He was embarrassed. "Well, yes, but I don't have time for the fancasts. I spend most of my time Gaming.

When I'm not Gaming I spend a lot of time watching Game episodes, but I don't pay much attention to the Gamers. I'm sorry. I hardly know who Walter Hauk is—fairly recent name, isn't he? Isn't he playing Donogon, king of the Doxons?''

"Oh, you should spend more time awake. Now that you're famous, enjoy it! How long before they want you back?''

Uneasily he said, "A couple of weeks, but they could extend that a week.''

"Is that all? I bet you could get a month if you wanted.''

"Well, they expect me back early, since I usually spend only a couple of weeks, so I suppose they wrote the Script to allow for it.''

"Believe me, these things are negotiable. Who are you?''

He laughed, shamefacedly. "I don't know. I have a sort of superstition against finding out. I suppose I feel that it would interfere with how I play the character.''

Judy nodded, leading him toward the punch bowl. On the stand, the musicians were lowering their weapons, as Thatcher whimsically thought of it. This was a very good public party; those were not bodies animated by computer programs, but by real live people.

"A lot of Gamers feel the same way.''

"Oh, Mr. Thatcher!'' A tug on his arm. "Would you—would you please autograph my breasts?''

Startled, Thatcher looked down. A small woman, a very neat package, hopefully bared, blinking long lashes up at him.

Judy smiled at his embarrassment, and when he stammered that he hadn't brought a pen with him, she turned to the crowd. Someone proffered a felt-tip pen. Thatcher looked blankly at the supplicant, then wrote "Andy K. Thatcher" on one breast.

It wasn't, he felt uneasily, Andy Thatcher they were seeing as they looked at him. It was Riandar, and Rollory, and all the others. With that wry thought, he turned to the other breast and slashed down the bold logo that indicated Riandar.

They were all delighted and Judy virtually had to bulldoze a way through the crowd. "Please, let the man have his drink! He's been dancing with *me*!"

The rest of the evening passed in a bright-lit blur to Thatcher. He remembered hundreds of shining faces, questions, names and address codes of men and women both, sprightly music, dances with Judy and other women, attempts to inveigle him aside. It was all a dream.

"Don't tell me," Judy said when they were alone in her hotel suite. "You've never experienced that kind of adulation? Don't you ever go out?"

"Well, not to public parties. I've never been socially adept, you see, and, well, I just never became a social animal. I have a few friends, of course—most of them Gamers, so I don't see them much—"

"And you spend all your time in the Game." She shook her head. "I'm going to have to introduce you to the pleasures of society—especially the pleasures of fame. But for now, come here and let's see if you're as good with that sword as everybody thinks . . . ."

* * *

Atlantis was an artificial island, partly floating on the sea and partly supported on great pillars. It was deeply convoluted, with many small pleasant bays, and had wide beaches all around. The topography was low, but there was both sufficient relief, and sufficient area, to create several sizable rivers. Judy took Thatcher to one of the small beaches next day and they did the classic lounging in the shade and the sun, swam, made sand castles, sailed a tiny boat on the little bay, inside the "reef" of the breakwater. Thatcher took the opportunity to work out, running and lifting rocks as well as swimming. While they did not have this cove to themselves, it was sparsely occupied, and no one disturbed them.

He was relieved, and a bit surprised. At breakfast he had seen this face on the newscast, heard the announcement that he was on Atlantis, and had seen views of the party last night.

The quiet morning was a mere respite, however. They were besieged at lunch at Ciano's, to Judy's proprietorial delight.

Ciano's was one of the most famed restaurants in the world; even Thatcher had heard of it. It was heavy with twentieth-century atmosphere: dim lighting, potted plants, a maitre d', waiters in suits and waitresses in modest ruffly dresses. Folded napkins with a border of cloth of gold, the tablecloths also with cloth-of-gold edging and cartouches. Jewel-encrusted candle lanterns at each place, lit with a flourish of the maitre d's hand. On the walls, prints of wild game birds and hunting dogs.

It would never have occurred to Thatcher, uncomfortable in a ruffled silk shirt and plum-colored suit, to come here, even now he knew that food was free. Surely one paid for the service? And this was indubitably human service, not computer-animated. But apparently there was no charge. He couldn't work it out; why would a live person animate a waitress, if there was no longer money in the world? They must be doing it for fun. But no doubt everybody not in the Game loved his or her job.

"I suppose this is what you mean by the pleasure of fame," he said to Judy, between the thirteenth and fourteenth fans who interrupted his meal.

"Surely! Part of it, anyway. Don't you enjoy it?"

He hardly knew. "It's all so new to me. But—I have the feeling it isn't *me* they're interested in, you know."

They were interrupted again, by a woman. The body was that of a young woman in her twenties, a brittle blonde beauty with a husky, sensuous voice. But her questioning was that of a different woman, and an image took form in Thatcher's mind: a plump, unattractive older woman with coarse skin and bulbous nose, a shrill intolerant voice. Innkeeper's wife type, he thought.

"I'm one of your *greatest* fans, Mr. Thatcher. I always said I'd do *anything* to meet you. I'm a great fan of the S&S Game; I play in it myself, you know. Just small parts now, but . . . ."

When she had gone, he said reflectively, "They all tell me they are Gamers. Practically everybody is, nowadays. So they know what it's like. Why do they think so much of me?"

"Well, that's obvious. They are bit players. Serving

wenches at country inns, innkeepers, assistant caravan masters, blacksmith's helpers, woodcarvers, and so on. *You're* special.''

The maitre d' approached to murmur a request: would the Mr. Thatcher be so kind as to leave a little memento for the staff—?

After lunch they went for a ramble in the interior of Atlantis. It was unspoiled; winding country roads between walls and fences thick with flowering vines; hidden fields, many of them fallow and in flowers; forest, glens and nooks artfully arranged; tangled hills; meadows. Late in the afternoon they stopped near the shore at a tiny, vine-covered inn much like those in the Games.

Judy remarked as much, laughing. ''Less likelihood of violence here, though,'' she added.

Thatcher grinned. ''Good thing. Despite this mountain I'm wearing, I doubt I'd be much help. I'd still be trying to introduce myself and shake hands when the swords began to sing.''

''Oh, here they are.''

Some of the men and women Judy had introduced him to last night were awaiting them; eagerly, by the expressions. Their names and address codes leaped to Thatcher's computer-assisted mind.

John Arronax, he thought, as he shook hands and murmured polite nothings. Judy must have been with him last night; she didn't know I was coming. Yet he did not seem jealous, to Thatcher's relief. He had scarcely been aware of the man last night. To his embarrassment now he heard Judy boasting of his, Thatcher's, prowess to the two women.

To Arronax, he said, deprecatingly, "Well, you know, if you've got a good Writer on the job and the computer is properly programmed," and turned red when they all laughed. Rather to his amazement they seemed not merely to admire him—he was beginning to get a little hardened to that—but to like him as well. Maybe this was the good side of fame that Judy had spoken of.

Arronax, he soon found, was quite a charming fellow, smoother socially than Thatcher of course, but not so smooth as to make him suspicious. They ordered wine—even Thatcher—and crab Rangoon, deerburgers and more wine, pan-fried fresh-caught young bass, a specialty of the house and still more wine. They were very merry.

That night Thatcher had to goad himself to do his two hours' workout, the bare minimum.

His first full day of fame . . . .

The next day, lunch at a small tavern on the beach turned into an impromptu party as the other patrons recognized him; they didn't get away till mid-afternoon. Thatcher's head was spinning pleasantly, but he was a little perturbed.

"Wasn't that fun?" Judy asked.

He assented, wondering, however, if he'd ever be able to do anything without interruption by his fans.

That night there was a lavish public party, and he had let her post his name as an attender. It was a costume party.

"You should go as Riandar!" Judy said.

"No, I couldn't. Riandar was a redhead."

Judy looked at him critically. "Or you could be a pirate, or maybe a warrior-king. Oh, I've got it! How about a prince?"

Thatcher was a little startled. "You mean a hero prince?"

"Well—why not just a regular prince, in a real fancy costume?"

Thatcher blinked, shaking his head automatically. "I've always done heroes," he said, uncertainly. For over a hundred years, ever since the era of primitive Gaming, he had played or aspired to play heroes.

He finally decided to go as Conan—the character was at least black-haired, though smaller than this huge body. The costume was simple enough, tight red silk trousers, bare chest and head, long straight sword, buskins. Judy went as a High Priestess of the Moon, a devotee of the love-goddess of Scensifer, in an outfit more erotic than nudity.

The party was in Fantasy Hall, a soaring yellow-marble building that looked like a Gothic cathedral, but was less "busy," not so ornate. Gothic made elegant. The interior was paler, warm straw-colored marble walls whose only elaboration were the moldings: gold arabesque traceries circling all the lofty rooms.

The party was a great success, with a number of notables from the various Games. Thatcher was the only S&S hero there, and was fairly mobbed with admirers. He did get to meet Carlos Rodriguez, who played great generals in the Romance Game—a man he had long admired. Further, he was introduced to Gunter Weintraub, the elvenlord player from the High Fantasy Game. Lucas

Brand Simcox, a well-known Writer for the Wild West Game was also there, who shook hands and told Thatcher he should try Westerns.

For the most part, though, he met fans. Thatcher was not drinking, but the lights, the dancing, and the fame itself, were dizzying. Halfway through the evening, feeling a weariness in his calves and feet, he reflected that he had totally forgotten to do his daily workout.

This was made up for when he was carried off by no fewer than three women, at the end of the evening. Sleep came late, and heavily.

It was after noon by the time they waked, roused, ate, and he had kissed them all good-bye, despite their wistful expressions.

Outside, he felt uncomfortable in his Conan costume, complete with sword. He was recognized and stopped several times by admirers and had to work to remain pleasant through the throbbing in his head. Might as well go ahead and drink, he reflected, if I'm going to get a fatigue hangover anyway.

Autographing, smiling woodenly, he had a brief fantasy of what Riandar might do: whip out the sword and lay about him, if only with the flat. Andy Thatcher couldn't do that, and if he tried, the computers would not transmit the commands to the body. No wonder people become soldiers in the Game, he thought, or mean guardsmen, or torturers.

At the first phone booth he called Judy. Pleasure and relief lit her features. "Oh, Andy! Have you had lunch yet?"

"Breakfast. Look, I'll be right up—there's a tube

station here. Uh, I'm sorry I abandoned you last night—''
Guiltily.

"Oh, that's all right! I hope you enjoyed yourself."

"Uh, yes. Look, give me a few minutes and I'll be there. Uh, we could go to the beach or something." The throbbing in his head faded, but he still felt guilty and wanted to make it up to her....

Under Judy's persuasion, Thatcher called S&S Game Central and extended his stay for the third week. He enjoyed the next two weeks very much.

Nearly every night, at one place or another in Atlantis, there was a public party which they attended. Judy was particular about posting them both as attenders; she never wanted to just drop in unexpectedly. Every day there was a lunch or dinner engagement with her and various of her friends or acquaintances. Gradually Thatcher came to realize that some of these acquaintances she had just met—met, he finally realized, on the strength of her association with him. And at these little affairs—often of as many as fifty people—the fan press was always evident.

It was fun, to sit and hold court over lunch or dinner, to be recognized when he went into a hotel or a restaurant. It was fun to meet the hundreds of true fans, and the thousands of celebrity-seekers, to sign autographs—he completely lost track of the number of breasts he autographed, but it was in the hundreds. He became quite blasé about it. This is fame, he would think.

Pursuit by women still perturbed him. He had come to Atlantis to spend the waking period with Judy, but one night in three he was inveigled away from her, unable to resist the pleading. He hated to hurt anyone's feelings, including those of newfound friends. Judy, to his relief, never seemed hurt, or jealous, and always seemed surprised when he returned.

No Game sequence had ever been so frantic, but it was all so much fun. Fun, if exhausting.

Two weeks of it did leave him very tired. One morning he stood observing himself somberly in the full-length mirror, nude. Judy came by when he was pounding his thighs and belly with his fists.

"What are you doing, Andy?"

"I'm getting flabby. Look at this—the belly is soft. Starting to stick out a little. I've got to get back in shape or I'll get myself killed."

"Oh, I wouldn't worry about that. A couple of days in the Game will toughen you up."

Thatcher looked at her. "I usually land in the middle of a battle. No, Judy, a fighting man is made, not born. The edge is off all my reflexes. I've got to start working out, and I'll need sword practice. Two hours a day is the bare minimum."

She was dismayed. "Two hours? There's hardly so much time—We have a dinner date with Armand and Enlai—And then there's the party tonight in Poseidonis—"

"I wouldn't want to disappoint Armand and Enlai, not to mention Ricia." Brightening, he added, "Maybe I should skip the party tonight."

"Oh, no, Andy! We're scheduled to be there—you wouldn't want to disappoint your fans."

Once that would have weighed heavily with him. Now

he hesitated. "How long will they be fans if I mess up in the Game?" he asked weakly.

In the end they compromised; he would spend an hour working out before the dinner, and leave the party early, to get some rest. Tomorrow he'd work out. He had made that resolution before . . .

At the party he was led to another celebrity, an Asian woman. Her body was that of a Mandarin Princess, all honey, amber, and black satin. "Tatyana Borisovna Gumilova," she murmured. "Your new Writer."

In his century of Gaming, Thatcher had never met his own Writer. Writers mostly lived in Australia, where the System's government was centered. Tatyana must have flown in by fractional-orbital gravship. As a dedicated Gamer, Thatcher knew the names of most of the S&S Writers; he had seen hers but only remembered one thing she had written. And that he had viewed, not read. That is, he was not familiar with her actual work, for the Gamers altered the script as they played it, within limits.

"So, I'll be playing in the Empire," he said. "—Don't tell me who my character is."

She smiled lazily up at him, looking like a panther in a relaxed moment. "The computers warned me not to. Right, you'll be in the Zhemrian Empire. You'll be playing a pivotal part. This is a more important role than usual for you; congratulations. And it's a step up for me, too, of course."

"Uh, did you ask for me, personally?"

"No, I didn't expect anyone so good," she said, giving him a meaningful look. "I just introduced the character they are giving you. Nobody could have predicted that Riandar would buy it just when he did."

"He had a good run," Thatcher said, trying to guess who his character could be. Big and black-haired. Oh no. He hoped they hadn't allowed the real Conan into the Game—custom excluded all the classic heroes.

They chatted about the Game, danced once, and the gleam in her eye excited him, but Thatcher's concern for Judy Somerset's feelings caused him to break away. And then he was dragooned by two women who wanted to hear about Riandar's last battle. He ended the night with them, recounting his battles and making rather languid love.

The next day he went to the nearest gym before calling Judy. Thatcher was alarmed and dismayed to realize how badly he had let himself go. Dancing, he reflected grimly, is inadequate exercise, sex even less so. And that was all he'd had for two weeks, despite his resolutions.

Feeling better if sore after his workout, he called Judy, and found her nearly frantic.

"Andy Thatcher, do you know what time it is? We have to meet Simon Cody for your interview in less than an hour! Then we have dinner with the Kungs and Nganga—"

"Better cancel the interview," Thatcher said. "I want to rest for a while, then do another hour at least. Otherwise, I'll tighten up."

"But—!"

"And dinner—I don't know about that."

"Tatyana Borisovna Gumilova will be there—your new Writer!"

Thatcher put his forearm on the phone screen, leaned his forehead on it. Tatyana's gleam had excited him. Even now he felt a pleasant thrill at the thought of her. But what he chiefly felt was weariness. He was not much interested in any woman. He was not much interested in anybody. What he wanted most of all was to plunge back into the Game. To cease to be himself.

"Judy, I've only got a week to get ready for the Game. I need a lot of sword practice .... Look, I'll call you later." No point in talking to her now.

He did make it to the interview, but skipped the dinner. Judy was coldly angry, but tried to contain it when he returned to the hotel after his second stint at the gym.

"You certainly left me holding the bag. Fortunately Tatyana was gracious. Andy, it's the first sign of temperament you've shown."

Thatcher shrugged, turned away.

"Okay, look, I'm sorry I lost my temper. Come on, let's get ready for the party. Tatyana will be there."

"I'm not going. I've got to sleep tonight. Tomorrow I've got to start sword practice."

She stared at him. "*Not going*? Andy, what is wrong with you? The Game is just a game! It's not important. This is real life—*this* is important!"

He stared back at her. "But *I'm* not important except as a Gamer hero! And I won't be one long if I blow it. I'm not really in shape for sword practice—but I've only got a week! I can't go to the party."

"Andy—"

He strode to the communicator and called the Public Office. "Andy K. Thatcher. Please announce that I will not make it to tonight's party. In fact, I won't be going to any more parties. I need to get in shape for the Game.''

''Yes, Mr. Thatcher. Do you wish to make a public announcement of that?''

''Yes, I do.''

Judy flung her hands up and ran out of the room. After a moment's hesitation, Thatcher left the suite. He walked at random for a quarter of an hour, then found himself near a tube station. He paused, considered calling her, then thought: later. . . .

The cool, quiet apartment in Tangier was an oasis. Thatcher stood looking around. It had not changed. He felt as he did when coming out of the Game and finding it unchanged; disengagement disorientation. Taking a deep breath, letting it out, he walked through the apartment, went to the phone. He had been in touch with such of his friends as were awake while in Atlantis, so had no new messages. Pouring a diet cola, he went and looked at the exercise machines.

Back in the living room, he said, ''Central, what's been happening in the Game in the past two weeks?'' He had quite lost track.

For the next week Thatcher stayed close to the apartment, working out on the machines, reading and watching Game records. Daily he went to a gym where he could do sword-practice against holos and computer-animated bodies. He was recognized there, but this gym was used by dedicated Gamers, who nodded but left him to himself.

Much of the time he spent brooding. Judy called him the next day. She was apologetic. ''I didn't mean to take over your life, Andy. It's just that I'm as starstruck as the next person. Next time we'll keep it quieter, huh?''

Against his better judgment, but unable to hurt her, he made a date to be awakened in four months.

Starstruck. It occurred to him that much as she enjoyed his company, much as she enjoyed sleeping with him, she enjoyed most being seen with him. Strange he hadn't realized.

Not all the women he'd met wanted merely to be seen with him. He remembered the ones who wanted to hear him talk about his battles, the bloodier the better. Especially while making love.

This had not occurred to him at the time. He *was* a professional fighter. His descriptions of the battles in fact were rather dry. For him they were first of all tactical exercises, then exercises in swordmanship, and his blow-by-blow accounts were nearly bloodless.

Still, many women were turned on by them.

Tatyana Borisovna Gumilova, he thought. That gleam in her eye. It wasn't Andy K. Thatcher who interested her; it was the character he'd been chosen to play. Someone she'd recently introduced into the Game. A fantasy figure . . .

The women in the Game—Slaves, Princesses, Priestesses, Tavern Wenches, and so on—were pure fantasy figures, and feminists had always decried them as sexist stereotypes. No more weird than the women he'd met in Atlantis, he thought, shaken. He preferred the Game women. They were more normal.

When the word came, it sent him to Ango. That was under the Congo—the Great Styx, or the Great River, in the Game. The Upper Empire; the northern and easternmost fringes of the Empire of the Zhemri, one of the largest on the Thurian Continent.

Pondering the politics of the Zhemrian Empire and trying vainly to guess what giant hero he could be on its scene, Thatcher went to the tube station.

3

The Battlefield Whereon
I Was Born

He awoke standing leaning back on a slant, struggling for breath. It came slowly through something dry and dusty over his mouth. It was very dark and silent. When he attempted to lift his hands to tear away the gag, they knocked against wood just in front of him. After a few minutes' strangling struggle his ready temper flared, fueled by panic, and he gave a convulsive buck, banging his head against the wood behind him and bringing his right knee sharply up into the wood before him.

It ripped away with a rotten sound, thudded to the floor, and a flood of ivory-colored light fell into his eyes, which were also covered. He panted quietly, hoping no one had heard the noise he had just made. In a moment he had torn the dry, crackling bandages from his face; he glared around the dusty chamber.

He was mummy-swaddled and mummy-coffined, but

this was no mummy tomb. It had been a public hall of some sort, high and wide. A palace or temple; the mummy case stood on a dais. The building had fallen in, there was a hole in the roof far above that let in a flood of yellow light, and a litter of sticks and leaves covered the dirty floor.

For a moment he was utterly confused, then memory returned with a flood. He was Taratan of the North, treacherously slain by the Wizard Humelin in Lurana long ago . . . . Long ago?

He shook off a feeling of confusion, as if this was something he'd learned by rote of a great hero long dead. Certainly it must have been long ago, he mused. The linen bandages were dry with age and the spices faded, the wood rotten. In a practiced gesture he slid his hand down the back of the mummy case beside him till it found the hilt of his great sword.

For a moment he tensed, blinking his eyes, expecting the light to brighten. Then he shook off the feeling angrily.

With all his barbarian caution Taratan had made no sound since freeing his face. Now he stepped warily out of the coffin, the linen ripping with dry brittle sounds. Surely he had been ensorceled by Humelin . . . now the last battle returned to him, dim as a dream an hour after waking, Humelin's face yellow and twisted, nose like a gnarled root . . . the Black Company's last wild, futile charge, its gallant doomed defense . . . himself ensorceled by Humelin and left for dead by all others. Brought here by Humelin in triumph. . . ?

His fingernails clear of the bandages, Taratan stripped

the dry wrappings from his sword. It had been oiled and the oil had caked the wrappings on the blade, protecting it. Taratan's heart sang at sight of that keen gray blade. Armed, he was dressed.

As he set about stripping the rest of the bandages off himself and forming a brittle loincloth of them, Taratan's eyes went to and fro. Nothing moved. The great hall was lifeless, its yellow marble, trimmed with lapis lazuli, dull and dirt-streaked.

From somewhere behind him came the sound of cold damp air sighing from deep caverns, a sigh that hinted at ghost whispers and caused the hair to prickle on the barbarian's neck. Looking that way, he saw a solid wall between him and the gulf whence came the sound.

Suddenly he knew where he was.

This was that city known to the Adepts of the Circle as Thuradroon, the Opening of the Way, and to the common people as the City of the Dead . . . whose basements gave on the halls of Hell itself. Only here would the Adepts have brought him at Humelin's urging, set up as an object of dishonor. Taratan snarled silently at the thought. But indeed it was long ago, for Thuradroon had perished utterly. None but lizards moved here.

That is how I was freed, he thought. Humelin must be dead and his sorcery with him, gone beyond vengeance, curse him! And the Adepts all dead too, the Circle broken down and all its works overthrown . . . freeing me as the spells faded.

All whom he had known were dead, then. It was as if he had but just been born, though fully grown.

For a moment, superstitiously eyeing the openings of

the room against the advent of some still-living Eater of the Dead in this City of the Dead, the barbarian had an uncomfortable feeling. Where had he been when he slept as if dead? Had his soul been where the souls of the dead go?

He seemed almost to remember scenes of violence and war, desperate struggles . . . a terrible battle not long ago against overwhelming odds.

Standing there, he felt suddenly not at all dismayed by the eerie happenstance of his awakening. It was as if this had happened to him many times before. *Where does the soul go when the body dies?*

Into another body as some would have it? How many lives had he lived while this his own body stood here, mocked by the Adepts?

A sound electrified Taratan as he stood, confused, disheartened.

In a moment forgetting his speculations and the dismay they had engendered, he gripped his sword, head on one side, listening. Yes! Pad of unshod feet, going unsteadily . . . whisper of painful breath.

In utter stillness Taratan sped through the crumbling corridors of Thuradroon the City of the Dead toward the sound, pausing minutes later to peer out a doorway toward a shaft of light from another hole in the palace roof. A woman fleeing recklessly toward him but near the end of her strength, he concluded. He waited and began to hear something of the sound of her pursuer . . . or pursuers.

As she came by his narrow door Taratan reached, swift as a panther snatching a hare, and pulled her in, his other hand going over her mouth. After one startled gasp and a kicking at the air as she was plucked running from her feet, she subsided. The barbarian recognized that she was still on the verge of a scream and rumbled, ''Easy, easy...''

Brown-haired, fine-boned, but tall and busty, with a full figure. A slave girl by her loin-string and breast binding and the earrings that—at least in old Lurana, which might be as dead as Thuradroon—had indicated a dancer and courtesan. Her breasts had bounced out of the binding, a golden silk band that complemented her skin. It had ridden up under her armpits. She put her hands to her chest and gulped air as silently as she could, staring at him big-eyed.

Taratan hadn't time for more than that glance. Whatever was chasing her was close enough to be seen if he had put his head out. Taratan listened intently. It was running fast, would probably streak right by his door before realizing it had lost the scent. It was big.

And by the sound of it, it wasn't human . . . .

Taratan stood with slitted eyes and sword at the ready, the girl behind him, all his futile speculations about death given over. Alert. Very much a part of this world's life . . . .

As it thudded toward his doorway, Taratan leaped out swinging his great gray sword. He had an instant's glimpse as he leaped. It was twice as tall as a man and had four feet. Then the sword bit home deeply into the right front knee and the back of a great hand struck him away.

In a lightning shift Taratan released the sword, stuck

firmly in the massive knee, and seized the wrist, looking up. A scowling, bestial yet humanlike face glared down at him. Then the scowl became a great cry of pain and rage as its knee buckled. Taratan bent the huge wrist, big as a man's leg, forcing the creature farther down. The thing's other hand flailed as it strove to regain its balance.

Amazed, Taratan looked at it from his wrestling hold. It was like nothing he had ever heard of. Its four legs were not mounted in pairs as he would have expected, but the right front a little in advance of the left, and right rear a little in advance of left rear, so that it came near stepping in its own tracks. He could see no reason for so odd an arrangement.

Whatever it was, or however it came to be, it suddenly struck at him with its near fist, jerking the other arm out of his grasp. Taratan released the wrist and ducked the left fist, leaping forward as it recovered from its backward jerk. In a moment his foot was braced against its ruined leg and his hands on the hilt of his sword.

A blow on his head from the massive fist nearly stunned Taratan, but he gave a mighty heave and the gory sword came clear. The creature cried out again, putting its hand in the blood on the floor and easing the leg. It looked at him with agonized gaze, put its bloody hand on the wall, and tried to straighten, shielding him off with its left.

In a moment he was hurtling toward it, in another he had checked, his bare feet gripping at the stones of the floor. It snatched a knife two feet long from its belt; the blades clanged together and Taratan was away. Then he was in again as it gaped, and he had sheared off the knife-wielding hand.

Death stared from its eyes, the stark certainty of its own death.

Regardless now of the pain in its leg, it threw itself upon him, blocking his sword with its wounded arm and seeking to bear him down beneath its own inevitable downfall. Taratan's sword glanced from the clublike arm and the thing's other arm whipped python-like around him, holding him in an unloving embrace.

The great coarse gray countenance lowered toward his face, teeth like granite tombstones questing for his life. Bracing his left arm against its throat, Taratan shortened his grip on the sword and drew it down. Ignoring a volley of blows from the handless left arm that sprayed him with blood, he stabbed and stabbed and stabbed upward into the thing's body, seeking its life.

For seconds the tableau held, till even the mighty barbarian's thews began to give way under the awful strain. The cords stood out in his left arm and neck, his teeth too were bared in a snarl not of savagery but of strain.

Then its fires sank and his arm began to push it away. The light in the thing's eyes wavered, dimmed, scummed over. Its blood was pouring about his knees and its bowels were slipping from its belly.

Taratan pushed it away and whirled in a complete circle with a flash of gray steel. Its head leaped through the air to bump and knock on the stones of the floor.

Panting, his muscles quivering from the release of strain, he looked about, belatedly remembering the girl.

She stood still in the side passage he had sprung from, pressed against the wall with her hand on her chest in the attitude he had left her, frozen. She stared at him wide-eyed with wild surmise.

"You slew it!" she whispered, still staring. "You slew the Hound of the Hunters!"

So that's what it was. Taratan took a deeper breath, said, "You need have no fear of me, lass. Who are you and what do you in ruined Thuradroon, the City of the Dead?"

"I-I am Ilantha. I w-was sent as a-a sacrifice to the Hunt. I volunteered, hoping—hoping to find my lost love, Rolodek, Prince of Zhemri. I expected only to join my lord in death. Oh, you have slain the Hound!"

Taratan glanced at the misshapen thing, dismissed it: "I caught it by surprise, but even so it was clumsy and slow. What hunt is this you speak of?"

Ilantha came hesitantly into the larger passage, looked in awe at the dead thing. She glanced superstitiously up at the light leaking through the hole above. "The Captive Hunt of Mohendro Sat," she said, her voice lowered. She came a little closer to the blood-smeared barbarian.

"Who are you, stranger, who prowl dead and haunted Thuradroon, slaying the members of the Hunt of the dread wizard?"

Even as he opened his mouth to reply, a deeper cunning than the barbarian normally knew opened its well somewhere inside him, drawing forth wisdom. "I am Jhillan," he said tersely.

That was the name of a talking tiger famed in song and story.

"Jhillan the Tiger," she said in awe. "I well believe it. But come! We must away ere the rest of the Hunt come upon us!"

"Away where?" he asked, not moving.

"We must find the Heart of the Serpent . . . the secret source of Mohendro Sat's power," she said. "It is whispered that here in this ancient city of sorcerers there is a room in which his heart is hidden. He cannot be slain so long as it beats on."

The keen hearing of the barbarian detected now, faint and far distant, a yammer of hellish voices. That well of wisdom opened again, emitting skepticism. "How is this known, if this wizard's hunt takes all who venture into Thuradroon?"

"It does not. Some among the slaves and guards whom Mohendro Sat employs have whispered of what they saw in this accursed city." Ilantha looked about nervously, not yet hearing the hunt, but fearing it. "Should we not go?"

The barbarian grunted, gestured with his sword. "Whence comes this hunt?"

"From the nighted gulf men call Esgalun, from a place that is said to be neither under nor above the good green earth, but beside it," she said, half trotting to keep up with him.

The ruined building they threaded was extensive but much of it was fallen in, many passages blocked with earth and stones. They came to a place where a great spill of earth and rock through a rent in the roof gave them a ladder up. On the roof, the barbarian looked about warily.

Green jungle gazed back, tree after tree in blazing sunlight all around. All were shrouded in clinging vines; shrubs and saplings blocked the view in every direction. Great tropical flowers peered at them from all around. It was hot and sultry; flies buzzed. The silence here was profound. Thurana was so long dead it was but barely visible as an occasional hummock beneath the trees. Taratan frowned. If Thuradroon were really abandoned long enough to sink thus into the jungle, how could the extensive rooms below have escaped being totally buried?

"Which way?" he asked.

Ilantha did not know. "The River lies west and south," she said dubiously.

It came to Taratan that Thuradroon must be somewhere in the wild, desolate—and demon-haunted—land of Almeria. If so, he knew generally where he was—hundreds of leagues from Lurana, if it still stood.

A sound electrified him. The Hunt's yammer, coming from a distance but above ground.

Ilantha heard it too and gasped. "Oh, what shall we do? You cannot fight them all alone—"

"Quiet!" Fiercely the barbarian listened, then thrust his head down into the room they had quitted. Even as the sound faded above, it grew louder below. "The Hunt just passed by another such hole as this," he said. "Come!"

They had passed several holes before finding one they could climb up to. Snatching up the woman, he ran fleetly and silently as the tiger, his new namesake, to the location of one of these. Scarcely had they concealed themselves and peered down, as into a well, than the Hunt passed.

Taratan heard Ilantha's shocked gasp.

The Hunt was a single creature with a hundred legs and a dozen, two dozen heads. Its many arms brandished all manner of weapons, chiefly crude clubs and spears. Its faces were cruel but of pronouncedly human cast. Awed, the barbarian guessed they were the semblances of victims eaten by the Hunt in the past, condemned now to hunt with the horror that had devoured them.

Even as he thought this he had a vision of the battle he must do with it. It would be dangerous to close with all those arms and weapons, but the creature must be slow on its feet. It would probably be necessary to lop off all those heads, and mayhap pierce its demoniac heart, he thought.

The Hound must have been a broken-off part of it. It occurred to him that the worst thing he could do would be to break its back. That was the obvious mode of attack.

Then from that cool well of wisdom within him came an answer. Battle was not the only, or even the best, way. . . .

"How far to the River?" he cried in sudden haste.

"Uh—eight or nine leagues, I believe," said Ilantha, startled.

"Too far!" But another similar plan sprang instantly to mind. "Come!" Snatching her up again, he sped across the jungle floor. "Where did you leave those who brought you here? How many of them were there?"

"There were perhaps a dozen of Mohendro Sat's dogs

who brought me from Lurana," she gasped, holding tightly to his corded neck. "They will be about the Gate, some furlongs to the west. They will not move till the Hunt returns to the gulf of Esgalun."

In moments, breathing hard, Taratan looked down another hole into the buried city. Before his long sleep he would have been in better shape, he thought resentfully. They had climbed a shallow slope, and now were looking down a depth of perhaps fifty feet, into that very hall of exhibition in which he had awakened. The hole here was not large, but it was by no means small; he kept Ilantha back from the edge, grunted, nodding, and fell to slashing at the limbs and saplings hereabout.

"Fortunately it's not rain forest, but all jungle," he said tersely. In a moment he had masked the edge of the hole.

And none too soon, for the multiple yelping and yammering of the Captive Hunt of Mohendro Sat resounded above the ground. One last chore with a vine—none grew in the proper place, so he had to swarm up a tree and tie one hastily but firmly in place.

When the Hunt burst into view a scant ten meters off, Taratan stood full in its view. Its aspect almost sickened the hardy barbarian, but as he had planned he gave a defiant yell and flung a rock. Then he turned and plunged into the growth behind him—seized the vine and swung across the masked hole.

Screaming cacophonously, the Hunt poured up the slope, tore into the fringing greenery—and screamed multiply as it plunged over the lip, and over, and over . . . .

And then there was an indescribably hideous multiplex thudding, as if of an avalanche of bodies into a well.

Taratan approached carefully, hearing a low pitiful moaning. Taking care of the crumbling lip, he peered down. After a moment his eyes adjusted and he saw the dying creature. Many of the heads still lived, and there was a strong throbbing in the central log of its body that boded ill for future victims. He suspected it could lose all of its "bodies" and start over anew.

"The heart must be slain," he whispered in awe to Ilantha. Again he had to climb trees and forcibly put the vines where he wanted them.

"Don't leave me alone up here!" Ilantha whispered frantically.

Taratan shrugged. "Climb on my back, then." He needed a hand for his sword and another for the vine. Wrapping the vine around his leg, he lowered them both into the depth.

Hideously, the killed multiple creature crawled implacably toward him even as its surviving conscious heads screamed in fear. Moving swiftly, Taratan lopped off its heads, putting who knows what innocent creatures out of their misery. Padding warily around it when he had done, he came too near the front end and belatedly realized that here was the controlling daimon of the thing.

Red-hot pincers seized his leg, a scorpion big as a dog struck him—no, a poisonous snake—

Taratan looked down through a red mist and saw that a jointed arm like that of an insect had seized his calf. It had in fact nearly missed, and the slightest movement would dislodge the paralyzing touch. But he could not make that move.

Through the buzzing in his ears Taratan was aware of a distant, a cold, an inhuman voice. A voice that told him that he had become the first head of the new Captive Hunt.

No, he protested inwardly, his eyes slits of agony.

Yes. You cannot resist. None can resist The Captor.

Taratan did not attempt to answer; he required all his mental force for resistance. Indeed, he could not have formulated the sound of his own name in his ears. All his concentration was required to maintain his individuality in the face of that monstrous and seductive sapping of his will to resist. For long moments he struggled, mind almost blanked to nothingness under that terrible pressure.

But Taratan's resistance checked and held on one stubborn rock. He was himself—thinking on a mere emotional level well below that on which names are used—and would remain himself.

And with that determination, the mind again took subconscious control of the body it could no longer sense. Dimly Taratan conceived of the idea of swinging a sword, as if it were an idle thought, or a distant dream. And it seemed to him that he remembered to have heard or dreamed that such a thing might have been done, somewhere, by someone, in a very slow and languid manner.

Stark scarlet pain slashed through his mind like a thousand screams in a thousand voices; Taratan's mind shimmered and wavered like silk in the wind. Then he was awake again and light entered into his again-seeing eyes. With a shake of his head, a sudden consciousness of terrible pain in his leg, that as suddenly ceased, he looked around.

He was again in the daised room where he had been exhibited in his trance. The Captive Hunt lay dead before him, his sword piercing the central red node at the waist of the first of the creatures that had composed it. From this node a jointed arm protruded. Even as he looked its tiny barbed jaws opened and it dropped from his leg, leaving twin marks like briar scratches.

Almost, the Captor had succeeded. What hellish spawn it was, from what part of the nighted Gulf of Esgalun it had come, or how Mohendro Sat acquired its alliance if not its adherence, could not be said.

Neither, however, could the demon dream of the depths of savage will from which the barbarian drew his resistance. Nor did it live to carry back to its dark home the warning to the others of its kind, if any there were, to be wary of barbarians such as this!

"Jhillan?" Ilantha cried. "What happened? You froze, and there was a look of dread on your face. You dropped your sword. Are you all right?"

"Yes. And it's dead; we need fear it no longer. Now we must deal with the dogs of Mohendro Sat, who brought you here. Or," he added, a new thought coming to him from deep within, "we might leave them to await word of your death, and seek out their boats on the River, stealing one and destroying the rest."

It was unsafe to leave an army unfought in their rear, yet as he thought it over, it seemed less and less so. No one could beat through the jungle as fast as a boat could drift downstream. And Lurana still stood, from what this girl said. It would be pleasant to drift down the River with her. . . .

But Ilantha said, "We must find my lord Prince Rolodek also, good Jhillan. Great will be the reward for the man who brings back the heir to the throne of the Empire."

Taratan bit the inside of his cheek as he considered this and reluctantly nodded. Appropriating a belt from the dead Hunt, he slid his gray sword through it and looked about uncertainly. Again he heard the rush of cold air from some nameless gulf back of the wall behind the dais.

"Perhaps here," he said.

After casting about in near darkness in several rooms for some minutes they found a place where the wall had crumbled. On the other side it was equally dark, and only Taratan's barbarian senses guided them toward the whisper of moving air. Presently he warned Ilantha; to their left was nothing—a gulf as dark and fathomless as Esgalun itself, it might have been.

Light appeared ahead of them and they went cautiously, found it leaking through a door. Beyond the door was another abandoned room, formerly used perhaps as a barrack, with one wall missing. It had fallen into the vast crack that had opened here in the earth beneath the City of the Dead.

Beyond the former barrack room was an ancient armory, now a hall of presence. In it lay, in a swaddle of green vines, a young, handsome, brown-skinned man.

"Prince Rolodek!" Ilantha cried.

Rolodek did not heed their presence; his eyes were pools of horror, looking out over the black gulf. Taratan approached slowly, looking at the vine with slitted eyes. It came up, thick and brown, out of that gulf, and its tiny, weak-seeming tendrils bound the prince. Bound him, and fed on him. They pierced his flesh and drank his blood. Sipped at it delicately, rather, came the cautionary second thought from deep within Taratan. It would quickly drain him dry if not.

"Oh, we must free him!" cried Ilantha. She ran forward to tear at the vine. Instantly the prince screamed and the vine began to thrash about—whether because of the prince's struggle, Taratan could not tell.

"No," he said. "Don't touch—"

Despairing, she screamed; it had seized her, too. Without bothering to tear her loose from it, Taratan sprang for the lip of the gulf and swung his great sword at its trunk. In the moment that his head protruded into the gulf, a wave of dizziness passed over him. He seemed to see suffering men and women plowing a vast, dry, cracked plain in blistering heat, under a red sky, under the lashes of black, batlike things. Then he was back, the vision gone, and the vine writhing in its death throes.

He turned to help the struggling man and woman free themselves from it, and paused. A tall, slender, dark man in a jeweled turban confronted him.

Taratan walked slowly toward him, face blank, sword held loosely but ready to deal death in any direction. "Mohendro Sat," he said. It was not a question.

It could never be a question with this man. "Indeed," said Mohendro Sat. "And you are—?"

The girl had become aware of them; she and the prince paused in their tearing at the vines. "Jhillan!" cried the girl.

"Seek not to deceive me as you have deceived this girl, my slave," said Mohendro Sat grimly. "For I know who you are. Each beat of your mighty heart thrusts your name unmistakably at me; I would know you in the dark. I would know you anywhere on earth, upon the mountains, in the desert, in the forest; I would know you on the sea or at the bottom of the sea. I would know you on the plains of Hell; indeed when next we meet, on those dry steppes, I will know you, Taratan of the Northriders."

Prince and girl both gasped.

Taratan took another step toward the wizard, moving half consciously. He was bemused to find he felt no fear of the other's sorcerous powers, now being readied against him. He was merely very curious about the man, and in a strange way regretted the necessity for killing him.

"Do you know what plot you have blundered into, barbarian?" the wizard asked. "This is no slave girl— this is Cyenia, Princess of the House of the Moon, affianced bride to Prince Rolodek, himself the heir of the Zhemrian throne. When she pretended to be a slave, hoping to rescue her beloved—"

Taratan was utterly bored by this. He decided abruptly, barbarian-like, to avoid Lurana, in fact to leave the Empire entirely. He would go north, he thought, back to the plains and forests of the Sahara.

Even while idly thinking thus, he leaped and swung his sword.

Startled, the wizard checked in mid-sentence and sprang clumsily back, astonishment written all over him. Grimly Taratan stalked him, till the other's upthrust palm stayed him.

"So! You dare to attack the Heir of the Ages! Know you not whom you confront? Know you not that I am the pupil of Humelin, who defeated you in ages agone? Know you not that I can blast you where you st—"

Again he avoided the sword with a desperate move, his back now to the dark gulf, and angrily bellowed a phrase Taratan could hear but not understand or remember. Taratan froze, paralyzed, raging.

The wizard straightened his clothes. He wore a gold-embroidered blue waistcoat under a light traveling cloak, and pants of a lighter blue, with gold piping. His turban, which he removed to straighten his hair, was foppishly feathered and laced, as well as jeweled, and there was lace at his wrists. Mohendro Sat was not the ascetic sort of wizard.

"Now your time is come, Taratan," he said, having recovered his equanimity. "Now you shall be sent to your long-deferred home. For a bat has flown across the Gulf of Esgalun and written the symbol that is your soul on the surface of the Pool of the Dark One. A wind came out of the Cave of the Dead and whispered your name in the ear of the Serpent of Endings. A skull has been burned black in the demonfire of Hither Hell and your name written in red on its brow—"

"That's ridiculous!" The feeling came from deep

within Taratan, and the barbarian, having no discretion, voiced it as he thought it. His impatient anger with this silliness freed him from the paralysis. Instantly he perceived this, he was in motion.

Again the wizard eluded his rush with a desperate movement, this time flinging powder into the air in his path. Taratan checked and tried to avoid the cast, but could not keep from inhaling it. The light vanished and his head spun round. He felt himself falling. He wondered if he had gone off the edge and was indeed falling into the gulf, or whether he had simply fallen in a swoon. Or both.

The darkness received him.

4

The Black Stranger

He awoke in ruby-lit darkness, gasping for breath. The wizard—the magic powder—the gulf of Esgalun—For a moment his heart throbbed convulsively and he flailed out with his arms. The he subsided, panting, relieved.

Decanted again. Something had gone wrong—he wasn't to be awakened for four months. And he was too small—this wasn't his body. What had happened there in Thuradroon?

Thatcher slid his hand down the side of the slantboard and light brightened around him. His hands were black. His knees and bare midriff were black. He was a blackamoor; probably a slave, judging by the skimpy loincloth—a body normally animated by a computer. He was probably the first man ever to animate it.

He wondered where his own Game body was.

When he opened the door he was confronted by a robo

doctor. This, he saw, was a small resurrection room, smelling strongly medical. There were a number of bodies moving about, all of socially inferior types like his current one, undoubtedly all animated by computers. The robo doctor of course was another animated body, with the universal robo doc face and the shiny bald head. It wore white med pants and blouse, but not the doctor's coat; there was a red cross over the heart. This one was a masculine body.

Thatcher smiled automatically, but said, "What happened, doc?"

"Analysis shows some interference, not screened out, from your mind, Mr. Thatcher," it said. "Apparently some of your own thoughts got through, thoughts foreign to the personality of your character."

Thatcher clearly recalled Taratan's irritation at the sensation of being herded helplessly in a given direction.

"But of course," he said, "my thoughts are Taratan's thoughts."

"To some degree that is true, sir. Let me give you a hand—you of course are not accustomed to this body. That's it, sir, just sit here." The slick plastic chair was cold on his bare buttocks. The table was apparently used for examining bodies; it had wheels and was segmented. "Perhaps some orange juice? I fear amenities are not up to the human norm here—this resurrection room is used only for computer-animated body processing."

"Quite all right. Something hot if you have it—coffee, perhaps." The air-conditioning here was cool. "Where are we?" Thatcher added.

"Memphis, sir." Cairo was not dismantled till the new

underground city was nearly completed, so they had used the old name for the new city. "When you crashed the system we had to switch you to the first available body. Not a very desirable one, I fear."

Thatcher smiled, gestured that aside. "I've played blacks before. I've even been a slave, twice. My characters have been enslaved, that is."

"Coffee, sir," said a female voice. A woman in a yellow smock approached from his left rear with a very plain, utilitarian cup balanced on a clipboard as on a tray. Tavern wench type; appropriate. "Careful; it's hot."

"Reverting to what you were saying, sir, about your thoughts being your character's thoughts," said the robo doctor. "That is true only to the extent that your thoughts correspond to those of your character. Improper thoughts must be edited out—such as, for instance, all those dealing with your true identity as Mr. Thatcher."

Thatcher sipped cautiously, nodded. "That's why people rarely play more than one type of character. If too many thoughts have to be edited out, the player is no longer animating the character."

"Quite so, sir. In your case, when I say that thoughts got through, I should have said, perhaps, that feelings got through. Taratan then spoke words corresponding to those feelings, but the words were not necessarily yours, sir."

Thatcher nodded. "Yes. Taratan is not me, nor the computer program that created him, nor the computer-editing function that links us with the body. He is a composite of all three." Every Gamer knew that, or should, though some preferred to forget, in their identification with the character.

"Yes, sir. Sir? My duties compel my presence elsewhere. As I gather you have no pressing medical needs, perhaps you could continue this conversation with Amaryllis? She knows all that I know."

"Certainly, certainly." Thatcher's mind was still on identity.

At this moment, with himself out of the circuit, the person who was Taratan literally had ceased to exist, as a triangle made of pencils ceases to exist as a triangle if one pencil is displaced. Somewhere, perhaps, Taratan's body was going through motions, under the control of the program; but the true, essential Taratan had ceased to exist.

A temporary death not much different from the empty span of time, three-quarters of a century, the character had spent in abeyance. During that time the character had not even had a body.

Thatcher shook his head, dizzy at the thought. Then he had another. "If a player gives up a character, and it is taken over by a different Gamer, the personality of the character changes," he said aloud. "So *this* Taratan never existed before, despite his memories of a past life." Setting his coffee cup down, he found that the examination table had a softer surface than it seemed.

Amaryllis seated herself opposite him and smiled. Curly brown hair, not as young as wenches usually were; perhaps she was the widowed proprietress of a small roadside tavern.

"Are you sure?" she asked. "The change, if any, is

very subtle, as the computers try to match player personalities with character personalities.''

''Yes, the change is usually subtle,'' Thatcher said.
''But sometimes it is marked, even among heroes, who
all have rather simple personalities.''

Breaking off, he said, ''Tell me, where is my body?
Taratan's, I mean. Did it fall into that—gulf?''

''Yes, that was the easiest way to bring the scene to a
close. I fear the gulf is more apparent than real. It's
less than a meter deep, the back wall is made of dull
black rock, and the floor is cushioned and covered with
black velvet. Whenever a character looks toward it we
edit out anything it might see, so that the gulf seems
vast.''

''And the rushing air was fan-forced, with the sound of
the fans edited out.'' Thatcher knew a lot about special
effects. He nodded. ''So Taratan fell unconscious there,
with the cushion muffling the sound of his fall into the
gulf, and is presumably falling yet. It'll be easy for the
Writers to extract him from that, and even drop him
anyplace they wish. The plot won't necessarily be altered
much.''

He wondered what Tatyana Borisovna Gumilova would
think.

''Have the Writers been notified?''

''They will be soon—it's only been a few minutes.
Your Writers are the third Writer's group for the Zhemrian
Empire.''

The computer-animated woman glanced away into the
bright-lit, orderly confusion of the resurrection room,
looked back. ''We're looking for a more suitable body

for you, sir, but so far without luck. I know people think we have unlimited bodies on hand, but that is because we usually have warning of the need for one. As you know, it takes almost two years to grow a new body and make sure the organic radio circuits are functioning.''

"It was over three years last I heard. Well, no problem; I don't mind wearing a slave body.''

Amaryllis appeared distressed. "Unfortunately, that body will be required soon in the Game—already we have delayed its entrance—and there wouldn't be time for you to go to Tangier and return. Logically, we should switch you back to your own Game body. However, that would entail considerable boredom and hardship for you.''

"Why?''

"The Taratan body is at this moment walking through the tunnels of Thuradroon toward an exit far from the Gate toward which Mohendro Sat is conducting Rolodek and Cyenia, the Princess of the House of the Moon. Unfortunately, Thuradroon is not a center of major activity, so there is no tube connection. The computer will have to walk him the rest of the day and more than half the night.''

There was no danger, of course. Characters in the Game, if there were any in that desolate region, would be steered away from him and he from them. And there were no large dangerous animals free on Earth; all the large animals in the forest were computer-animated. They lived perfectly normal animal lives most of the time.

"It does sound boring,'' Thatcher said. He sipped his

coffee; it had cooled. "So I just have to sit here and wait?"

She seemed embarrassed. "Well, sir, no, that won't be necessary. There are a number of possible entertainments in Memphis. You could find a public party, or a restaurant or tavern. Perhaps a gaming club. Or for that matter, you could go up. Memphis is under the Kingdom of Darfar, you know. The city of Darfarism is just overhead. It has a number of taverns, the pyramid tour, and so on."

"In the body of a slave?" he asked, blinking.

"There is a tour group."

It did sound better to him than public parties where he knew no one, or strange Game clubs. He had never beheld a Game environment with his waking eyes.

"The tour group sounds interesting." he said.

Twenty minutes later, Thatcher climbed an ancient, dank stone stair from the deep cellars of a tavern, up from the tubeway. The heat of Egypt mounted as he climbed. He was wearing the vest, buskins, cap, and slit skirt over his loincloth that denoted a slave to a middle-class family in Darfar, in the Game.

"Ho! Rantus! You lazy black dog, hurry with that beer!"

Despite the shout, Thatcher paused in order to repress firmly his knowledge that he was in Egypt, on the site of ancient Memphis of the Pyramids. This was Darfarism, and across the River were not the Egyptian Pyramids, but the Fanes of the Greater Gods. The River was not the Nile, but the Feathered Serpent. That always caused Thatcher to frown. A purist, he held that American

Indian references should be omitted from the S&S Game, which was based on European histo-mythology.

"Rantus!"

The innkeeper's name was Fan Fanych, he knew; a gross, belligerent, scowling sort, but not particularly brutal. A computer-animation. Thatcher hurried, scuttling rather clumsily, with the glazed earthen pitcher. He should have spent some time working out with this body, as his reflexes had been reset for the huge frame of Taratan. He did not trip or spill anything, though.

The inn was of massive construction, some stone for sturdiness, but mostly mud brick. It had been whitewashed about the time the Fanes were built, and the whitewash that remained had several layers of dirt in sedimentary deposits over it. Woven reed screens in native golden-brown over the windows added a pleasing touch, and shut out the blasting heat and light. Similar screens were stood up before the doors in typical Darfar fashion; a whole row of them along the west protected the building from the ardent sun.

The table of his people was outside, under a woven reed awning, this one painted not too long ago, red and gold. Dodging past the scowling Fan Fanych, he hurried obsequiously as he could to the table and poured carefully. There were eight of them, gaudily dressed in white turbans with gold cords, ostrich feathers for the women. The men wore ballooning pantaloons with gold-embroidered sashes; the women wore gold-embroidered caftans. The pantaloons were white, but the shirts and caftans were turquoise and scarlet, aquamarine and violet, every shade in fact but the mild or pale.

"So we have a slave now," said one of the young women of the party. "You're a real person too, we understand."

"Yes. Call me Andy," he said in a murmur. There were probably none but waking people or computer-animations within hearing, but it was best to be careful.

"Nice body, Andy; you look just like a slave ought to look," said the older man who seemed to head the party. This was allegedly a family group; actually they were a club or something.

"Pour one for yourself, Rantus," one of the two young men urged him.

"No, no," said Thatcher, seconding the strong negative that welled up in his computer link. "Don't be democratic; Darfar is class-stratified and racist to boot. I'll drink what's in the bottom of the pitcher, same as slaves always do."

The whole party laughed at this and he made his escape, the internal urgings of the computer link guiding him, as it had guided his steps on the dance floor. In the dark hall between the kitchen and cellar stairs, he did indeed drink the dregs of the pitcher, smacked his lips loudly to provoke a roar from the outraged Fan Fanych, then hurried on down to deposit the pitcher by the bung.

As he neared the top of the stairs, Fan Fanych was again bellowing at him: "See to your people, you lazy scut!"

They wanted nothing, of course; but no slave should be left more than a moment in a place full of wine and beer. Thatcher gave the innkeeper a wide grin and faked a hiccup, causing the other to take on an apoplectic appearance.

"Rantus," said the patriarch of his party—the name Polondar welled up in Andy's mind—"we mean to cross the Serpent and tour the Greater Fane. Here—" tossing him a purse. "Go procure passage and arrange all needful things."

Fan Fanych immediately became alert, and moved on him. Thatcher considered that if he did not patronize the other, the innkeeper would attempt to cheat "his" family.

"I can arrange all!" said Fan Fanych quietly to him. "Rantus, listen, for twenty-four shekels I can arrange passage and entrance and food, complete with bribe to the lesser priest. We'll tell your patron it cost twenty-eight, and split the difference. Eh? What do you say, my man?"

"This unworthy black dog says fuck off, white man. What! Am I to cheat my good master and mistress for a piece of white trash? My mistress that sat up beside me and nursed me with her own hands when I was so sick I thought she was my mother? Not a groat more than eighteen shekels."

Purple, the innkeeper kept his voice down. "Twenty-two, then, you bastard. I've got to show *some* profit. I have to split with the boatman, too, you know."

Enjoying his power, Thatcher said, "Nineteen, and that's my final word."

"For a ha'pence I'd squeeze your scrannel throat shut! Twenty."

"No you wouldn't; did anyone offer you so little, you'd immediately try to chisel more. Done at twenty."

Fan Fanych barked a startled laugh, extended his hand. But his good humor reverted to scowling when Thatcher refused to pay over the money.

Thatcher said, "I come along."

Grumbling, the innkeeper led him to a ramshackle wharf where a ramshackle boat swung idly to a half-rotten cord. Under a ramshackle hut slept a ramshackle boatman. He looked like a skinny version of Fanych and was probably a half-witted cousin. Fanych proceeded to beat him down on his fee, paid him a shilling on it, and told him to wait. The half-wit crawled back into his shed.

"I will send a boy to the Fane," said the innkeeper, rubbing his hands together. "You can pay me now."

"You will send me with him, or get no money," said Thatcher.

Fanych cursed and raved and finally broke down. "Why send anyone? Even my half-witted nephew charges at least a half shilling per crossing, whether his boat be light or heavy. You can run ahead of your party and make the arrangements. See, I will give you a signet, to show to Mamand, the priest, who will let you into the Fane for but five shekels the party, I swear it!"

"Any more than that which he charges shall come out of your portion, then," Thatcher said.

"Well, it may be that greed will drive the little bastard, and he will seek to mulct you of seven or it may be eight shekels."

"More likely ten, but even eight shekels I find easier to believe."

As they returned to the inn, Thatcher repressed his grin with difficulty. So this was life from the underside, or rather, this was the Game from the underside. Now he understood why people liked it. There was something appealing in matching wits with destiny, something perhaps as heroic as hacking one's way through. Furthermore, a servant could take pride in a job well done, as much as any swordsman's pride in his sword art.

He wished now that he *had* gone to that party in Atlantis dressed as something other than a Hero, as Judy had suggested.

At the inn, Thatcher gathered up his party and conducted them to the Serpent. The boatman found spaces for them all and provided another oar for Thatcher. Though the boat was deeply laden, it bore them over the calm water well enough, and after a long sweaty trip, about two kilometers, they touched at a landing near the Fanes.

Swarms of bearers descended upon them, and Thatcher beat them off with the oar, ordering them to fall into line, while his party stood grandly behind. One bearer had a fine riding mare, the product of some proud stable, but badly scarred on the knees and chest, probably in a fall. Her he allotted to the patriarch, Polondar. For the matriarch and the daughter, a capacious sedan chair; for the other two young women, another. For the three young men he got the three most spirited burros. Finally, he hired the least ruffianly looking guide, ostensibly to lead them; actually to protect them from other brigands selling their services.

He ran on ahead, the sedan-chairs slowing the party to a sedate pace. Once he had a proper lead, he slowed to a walk, panting. It was a goodly distance, but a fast walk would keep him ahead of his party. The way led for kilometers over an elevated causeway, which Thatcher remembered from the time Akanax had been in Darfarism long ago. The causeway was longer now; or was it that he had been riding then?

The Pyramids loomed above the palm trees, but he could not watch them grow, for he had to avoid anyone on horseback. As a slave, he would simply have been ridden down if he got in the way. At length he climbed the last steep slope, the sun beating down, and felt the breath of air blowing toward the Sea of Nasser, the flooded bed of the old Qattara Depression. In the Game it was called the Sea of Votishal. Clouds billowed tall above it, visible though far away.

Here where the desert once stood, grim and uncompromising, glaring down at the Nile, now the great plains of Amara swept west toward the forest that bounded the Sea. Wiping sweat, Thatcher came up to the wall around the Pyramid of Khufu, or Cheops. He stood and waited while ten people approached the little wicket in the gatehouse, some of whom had arrived after he had. Finally there came a break in the flow of free people, and he crept to the wicket.

"Fan Fanych desires that his friend Mamand will grant permission for eight of his guests and their slave to visit the Great Fane," he said, showing the signet and clinking coin in the sack in his pouch suggestively.

The automatic scowl on the other's face, at sight of a

slave, faded. He looked thoughtful. "I am Mamand, dog," said he. "And the number of admissions is complete for the day: none more may enter."

"My master will be disappointed," said Thatcher, clinking the money and turning reluctantly away.

By the time his party arrived, Thatcher had acquired the admissions for a fair price and was still bending himself double at the wicket in thanks.

Seeing the state in which the party rode, Mamand (if it were he and not merely another priest getting in on his graft) came out and opened the gate himself. The priest bellowed for an attendant to take his place and led them about the temenos, lecturing them the while on the Great Gods and the purpose of the various parts of the Fane.

Thatcher paid little attention to this. The Pyramids had been opened thoroughly, cosmic-ray scatter photography having shown all the rooms and passages. It was little touched by the Game. That was a part of the agreement that opened Egypt to the gamers; the alternative had been to dismantle the Pyramids and move them all to Australia. Even so, in the new, wet climate of North Africa, the stone would have eroded if it had not been coated. They went through it, paying only marginal attention to the priest's lecture, for the Pyramid had but little to do with the mock religion and temple that had been built around it.

The priest wanted to take them all over the temenos; the complex included not merely the Great Pyramid but half a dozen smaller buildings within the wall, all built for the Game and quite meaningless. They begged off, to the priest's irritation—he was, Thatcher was sure, a character and not a computer-animation—and finally got away.

"Shall we go through the Lesser Fanes?" Polondar asked.

Their compounds were nearby. But the group was tired.

"Back to Darfarism it is, then!"

This time Thatcher followed them obsequiously. His slave body was sturdy, but he was tired by the time they'd recrossed the Serpent and were wending their way through Darfarism.

At one point they were held up by a procession of yelling, laughing, gesticulating natives following a death march—a man on his way to the headsman's block. The look of horror on the victim's face was a treasure—he was obviously a character, and of course execution was the death of the character, so the look of horror was appropriate.

Thatcher had twice nearly been run over by horsemen who seemed not even to have seen him; he found himself more sympathetic to the victim than he would have been at any other time in his life. Heroes killed criminals and other designated villains, not sympathized with them.

The thick walls of the inn were a refuge from more than the heat.

Subsequently Polondar rather apologetically sent him out to buy several items the family wanted. Thatcher went gladly, pleased to get away from the heavy atmosphere around Fan Fanych. The first merchant he dealt with, a dealer in old crockery, cheated him. He had bought merely a pair of small soap trays, so the sum involved was ridiculous, yet it was obvious that the other had cheated him and would report him as a thief if he so much as protested.

Indeed, the other was obviously half minded to report him anyway, for the hell of it. Only the heat and its being the end of a long, hot, tiring day saved Thatcher.

As a slave, of course, his testimony would not even be taken, and while there was another free man or two in the area, it was impossible, from their laughter, to believe that they would big-heartedly come forward and testify in his defense. Rather the reverse.

At the next merchant's, one who dealt in old cloth, he was nearly involved in a fight. A bored young man, who had apparently spent the day cleaning out a cistern, or several, shoved him, called him a black dog, the son of a black she-camel, and from there became insulting.

Thatcher burned with rage, but to so much as lift his hand in defense could get him executed. The merchant, blaming him for everything, chased them away, and the youth was too tired and hot to follow him. He got the cloth at a different merchant's, and started for the inn.

His natural first reflection was on the numerous people like the obnoxious crockery merchant and the obnoxious cistern cleaner whom he had killed in his various incarnations; for instance, as Akanax, in Darfarism. That made him feel a little better. For lifetimes now, when Thatcher walked such streets as these, people had looked on him with respect; even with fear.

Brooding thus, he nearly walked into a fight between watermen, polers of rival barges, deadly enemies for their attempts to steal cargoes from each other. Then he realized that it was several from one boat who'd caught one from the other. The victim was in a fair way to be killed, as his expression showed. He got free and backed against the wall of a mud hut, eyes wild, knife in one hand.

Riandar might have rescued him, or Taratan. Rollory certainly would, Akanax maybe. Thatcher as Thatcher-pretending-to-be-Rantus hadn't the slightest inclination to try it. Yet he felt most strongly for the poor fellow. Ultimately the City Guard came, tramping importantly in rawhide boots and swinging billhooks. All but the dwellers in the nearby huts ran, and the dwellers looked innocent.

Running away was a new experience. So was this pounding heart. Fear. Thatcher had not known such fear since very early in the Game, before he attained the status that brought him the better bodies and juicier roles. He'd been a city watchman himself, many a time—boring role—and a hired guard. Still, even then he'd had weapons and had been free, not a despised slave.

At this point, with the inn before him and the prospect of Fan Fanych's scowl, Thatcher remembered that most of the slaves in the Game were computer-animated. So were most of the serfs and peasants—there were occasional Gamers who played such roles, but they were rare. Only the oppressors, the merchants and the watch and even perhaps the cistern-cleaner, were real people. The boatmen, too, of course.

The verisimilitude of the Game was legendary. Even the biggest building here was built by bodies hacking away at rocks with hand tools, pulling and hauling in the ancient ways. But the laborers who sweated in the sun usually weren't real people.

With ruthless Game logic it had been decreed that such societies as were normally depicted in the S&S literature from which the Game derived would naturally have crime. That meant criminals, a police system, a criminal court system (quaintly corrupt, of course), and brutal punishments for crime. But only the dashing and romantic criminals were real people; the lowlier ones were all computer-animated.

When tortured and killed, their bodies died rather as meat than as people. The bodies used in the Games were gene altered and had scarcely enough brains to keep their hearts beating and lungs working. Turtles—worms—had more individuality—more life. The big brain-pans were filled with the organic signal apparatus whose antenna leads took the form of special nerves running along the arms and legs.

Still he felt oppressed.

Out here in the sun it wasn't merely the heat that was oppressive. "Rantus! Rantus! Your party wants you! Get your lazy black hide in there—"

Possibly the computer behind Fan Fanych's scowl wondered why Rantus smiled so scintillantly at him.

Thatcher was very tired when he curled up in Rantus's little cubbyhole under the eaves of the inn that night. Curled up, slept, and dreamed.

He was in Darfarism again—the Great Pyramid loomed

above the city as it did not in reality, being across the
River—and Thatcher ran. Thatcher was Rantus, the skinny
miserable black slave, who tore off his cap and vest and
slit skirt to pacify the screaming mob of poor Darfarians,
as if to say, "See! I do not set myself above you, though
my masters are rich and kind!"

But they did not listen, only screamed the more hatefully
at him. Panting, Rantus looked back, and saw the beheaded
man leading them, holding his head high on a hod, with
the cistern-cleaner and the waterman next. Behind, the
cloth merchant and the crockery merchant.

He had let himself be pursued into a dead-end. Thatcher
leaned against a rickety, sloping door, trembling and
panting. In desperation he slid his hand down the side of
the slantboard, hearing fumbling at the door behind him,
and slid the light switch. Supplanting the ruby red of
fear, came white light.

He was tall. He was big. He was a hero. He was
Taratan with a face made out of iron and a jaw like the
prow of a carack.

Fists beat on the door behind him; the pursuing mob
came around the corner, and now they were the people at
the party in Atlantis. They were all beautiful and upper
class and civilized and high in Game status. Every one of
them knew how small he, Thatcher, really was and
despised him. Taratan was in an utter panic.

Turning, he fumbled the door open and leaped into
darkness, trampling over someone who squealed and bit
at his leg. He slapped her off as he would a mosquito,
careless of the blood, and ran through cluttered darkness,

heart pounding, head spinning, feet stumbling, not yet sure of his steps in the big body.

He looked back at the door where all the light in the world was, and it was Judy Somerset who showed them the way to him.

5

One Sought Adventure

With a gasping effort Thatcher shook off the horror of
the dream and jerked himself into waking. He realized in
the first movement that he was back again in his "own,"
his Taratan, body. Relief flooded him. Ridiculous, he
thought, to be so terrified of a dream. Still more ridiculous that a reality-experience should work on him so
powerfully as to cause such a nightmare.

Perhaps not, he thought, broodingly.

YOU ARE IN THE TUBE, NORTHBOUND TO TAN-
GIER FROM ANGO. The thought was from the computer
that monitored the flow of feelings and thoughts between
animated and animating bodies. They rarely intruded in
such manner.

Thank you, computer, he thought deliberately at it.

It occurred to him belatedly that he was not in a public
place and might be recognized as Taratan/Thatcher. He

quickly resolved to pretend to be a computer bringing the body back, then he thought: the Privacy Act, of course.

Computer, he thought. *I request protection under the Privacy Act.*

GRANTED.

From now on, he knew, anyone who looked at him would see a tan-colored blur where he was, and the looker would be uncertain even of what size he was. Thatcher slumped.

The nightmare....Thatcher had now been playing invincible heroes for longer than he had been alive when he first got into the Game. But the early days of a person's life leave the deeper marks. He'd been a helpless little muppet then, and knew it—still knew it.

Fear of being helpless, he thought. He stretched, trying to find room to relax in a world made for smaller frames. He considered asking the computer to wake him if he had another nightmare, decided against it. . . . A restful time later he awoke and immediately knew that he was alone in an empty car that was parked in a holding area, patiently waiting for him to awaken. In Tangier.

The city had not changed while he was in Darfarism. Of course it hadn't. It was he who had changed, Thatcher thought. . . . Cool and quiet and brightly lit in the major ways, dim and peaceful in the quieter places, a city of soaring, heartbreaking beauty underground, a city of the pattern of heaven: a place of no crime, no corruption, of no oppression or misery, a city where poverty had no meaning, or vice. A city empty, or nearly so: the inhabitants were mostly out killing each other in the Game.

His apartment had not changed either. At least Thatcher

could get rid of these damned aged-linen rags. Donning less scratchy underwear, he trailed out into the living room, feeling wired. His computerized internal time sense told him it was early in the morning, his stomach that it was past breakfast.

There was an answer from Erika, who was now awake. He called her. Erika was now a small, dark, elfin woman; in all her bodies she had a characteristic turn to her eyelid and nose, interesting, exotic.

"You just caught me, Andy—something happened in the Game, right? There was a news squib; you're quite the lion now. I suppose because of your conquest of Atlantis. You couldn't have more respect if you had done that with a sword. Look, I'm dying of hunger and you know my views on barbaric function rooms. See you at the Underfront? How about the Grotto View III?"

The Grotto was impressive, with its waste of water rolling away out of sight among the transparent columns. Where water met land was the bathtub-ring of the Underfront.

The Grotto View III knew them, and they got a good table. Thatcher was still under Privacy Lock—the computer-animated waiter was allowed to see him, but carefully called him "Mr. Andy."

Erika had just gotten in. She nodded pleasantly at him, not at all as if this was the first time they'd met in a year, indicated the Underfront and made a remark about their splashing about on it most of a century ago.

It was breakfast for both of them, and Thatcher had Taratan's appetite. He ordered ham, eggs, bacon, sausages, hash brown potatoes, pita bread, and baklava.

"And your strongest Turkish coffee with plenty of milk. No cream."

Erika snorted. "Think the low-calorie milk will offset all that grease? Two of your poached brook trout; oatmeal, with milk, no sugar; Spanish-style chicory decaf, black; whole-wheat toast. And baklava." To Thatcher: "So how've you been? What happened in Thuradroon?"

"That was really quite comical. A few of my own feelings got though the link. You know, John Wendell Wei may not have liked Riandar much, but at least he wrote him competently."

Erika grimaced. "By Crom, call *Ice Post Zero* competent? Wei can't string four words together without committing one cliché."

"True, the writing as writing may be bad, but the character is always handled solidly. Wei understood him. I think Taratan needs a stronger component of doubt. He's not so credulous as my usual character."

"Yes, your characters do tend toward sterling worth rather than brains. Hmm. A bit more of a cynic. Might make a note to the computer to post your Writer—Tatyana Borisovna Gumilova?"

"Yes."

Erika pursed her lips. "She's *good*." Andy nodded; Erika said the same about all women. "I met her once, and she certainly impressed me. I heard her taking apart a Majippor script for the Oceanic Games. *Very* impressive."

That she didn't often say, and Thatcher sat up.

"You could tell she knew the Game well, and she had mastered the backgrounds and foregrounds a lot better than anyone not in it would think."

"Yes?"

"So, this woman is taking a personal interest in your character. That happened to you with Rollory, didn't it?"

"God, yes."

It was the trial of a player's life, to have a Writer take an interest in one's character. Even a friendly interest. The first thing they always wanted to do was to change the character, and very few Writers (who seemed able to write any kind of character) could understand that Gamers didn't work that way.

"She asked for Taratan specifically in this Script." Thatcher shook his head.

Food was delivered, interrupting momentarily, and he began to eat hungrily. As usual it was excellent. "Taratan apparently means something to her. That's bound to affect how she writes him."

"You should ask at the very least for her conception of the character, and of course the memos the computer has on file for the last several concepts."

"Good thinking. Damn, I'm a bit rusty at this. Do you realize, Erika, that I haven't had a Writer problem since that one with Rollory?

"No one else in the group has either. Of course at our ages we're naturally going to be pretty set in our ways. They don't waste time fighting us. And to give you a well-deserved Nod, Andy, I think you've been doing real well in a specialized and highly competitive field. Of course that Nod will have to be ratified by Clancy."

Thatcher expanded his chest remarkably. "You have no idea how much that means to me. Indeed, I shall ever treasure this humble and powerful moment; whether I dare aspire to the Nod itself or not, I know that—''

They ended at her studio, or, better, boudoir apartment, where they had a rowdy time as befit old friends with no entangling alliances or clashing sexual preferences. Another friend, Delain, dropped by later that evening. Andy exuberantly exhibited his new body, posed in all the classic sand-kicking postures (including erect, with Erika), and Delain took pictures. A stranger would have thought them all drunk, but a stranger would not have understood their slangy, salty speech with its allusions to their century together.

"When I saw that bod on the wall, I thought, I believe the kid's done it." said Delain. He was currently a wild-eyed, merry grig of a blond boy who looked like a minstrel but was actually a thief. He had no ear for music—it sharpened the Game for him to give himself some such pitfall, and he made sure the computers and Writers knew not to edit in that function.

"Yeah," said Erika. "You've probably got the closest approach of fame any of us will ever get. I suppose if you stay in high social circles you'll continue to be famous."

"Unless I take a shellacking in the Game," Thatcher added complacently.

The next night, such of the full group as were awake bounded through the door of a large hotel suite. Thatcher had informed them all of the right to free housing, and Erika immediately took that up with the computer. The result was this suite, which he supposed would have cost some hundreds of dollars a day in the old days. It looked like a futuristic home upholstered by a sultan.

Thatcher got his Nod, delivered duly and with all solemnity by Clancy. She was a cross-dresser who almost always played men.

Delain, the impish thief, said, "Let's all line up and Nod at him simultaneously."

Clancy said, with dignity, "The Nod can in no way be compromised. We live in a world which has debased its gauds enough as it is. *The Nod*, you may rest assured, will never be altered."

And Delain was duly ejected.

With typical house-holders' regard for thievery, the group posted a guard on the front door, didn't think about the back door. Delain could have re-entered readily, disdained to do so. He had to hold his end up all by himself, going round through the emergency escape and persuading the humorless computer that it was a joke.

"Some Gamers *you* are!" he told them, scrambling in through the escape hatch.

Next morning Thatcher had a recorded message on his telephone from Tatyana Borisovna Gumilova, back in Australia. She was as beautiful as ever, but mercifully businesslike. Oddly, she apologized to him for the problem. It was her intention to reinsert him into the Game at Lurana, the Zhemrian capital. She thought she would bring Taratan and the Zhemrian factions into contact, after which she could let some aspects "coast."

Thatcher nodded. In effect, coasting meant that the

Gamers and the computers wrote the story on momentum, reacting to each other as their characters dictated.

Tasha wanted him there at Lurana in six days. He would awaken in the crumbling fane of Lric, a dead hero deified, but who had never been allowed into the Game because of racism. Good enough. Presumably all these god places connected, the Gulf of Esgalun and Lric's fane. Eight ball in the side pocket. Thatcher laughed, wondered if there were still an active pool or billiards table on Earth, and called her. Fortunately it was night in Australia and Tasha was not receiving; asleep or out. Better not to feed her fantasies of him/Taratan.

Lurana, capital of Zhemria! From a city of mud huts with thatched roofs to a city of marble, how it had grown, and was still growing. Hod-carriers outnumbered the numerous soldiers. Taratan stood looking out on it in wonder. How had he come here—here to Zhemria, where he was meant to be?

With a wary look behind at the unhumanly shaped statue, he slung his sword through the rope that upheld the dusty altar cloth he had found in the fane. Taratan slipped out into the street with the stealth of the panther, the silken grace of the cheetah. People stared. Even in the barbaric, raw blood and gold capital of the great Empire, seven-foot-tall adventurers wearing dusty purple kilts and bare blades require explanation. He had best avoid the Watch.

However, traffic moved fast in this busy capital, and a cluster of people bore down on him before he could avoid them. Not to worry, they saw him and scattered, one dropping a cabbage into the mud. But right behind them was a black slave. He saw Taratan too late, tried to leap aside, spilled wine on him, and fell, still trying to hold level the wine bottle, half his size. He stared up at Taratan in agony.

Spilling that wine might cause a short-tempered master to kill a nearly valueless slave. Spilling wine on an armed man in the capital of an expanding empire might mean immediate death, forget about master.

Taratan leaped forward, caught the vessel, and lifted it off. "Here, you fellow," he said to one of the bystanders— one so lowly it would not degrade him to touch a slave. "You hold this and I'll get him up—Well, take it, you ninny, or I'll smash it over your head—"

Quakingly the other obeyed, and Taratan turned back to the still-gaping slave. That worthy thought rather slowly or he would have been on his feet by now. It apparently hit him all at once that Taratan meant what he said about helping him up, but before he could move, Taratan had a mighty paw on him and he was dangling well above ground. The fellow seemed too bemused to notice that he wasn't standing. Taratan let him dangle closer to the ground, frowning, and finally decided he would stand if all support were withdrawn.

This experiment a success, Taratan said in irritation to the murmuring mob, "All right, show's over. Be on about your business."

He turned to the fellow with the wine bottle, which he was allowing to rest on the mud, gaping in fascination at Taratan. The bottle was nearly four feet tall, with a flaring rim, in brilliant black and red and gold. Taratan glanced at it in irritation—what kind of a thing was it?

"Right, give it to him." Gesturing to the slave.

The murmur of the crowd ceased. Nobody moved. It was as if a spell had been laid on them all.

The slave recovered first, stepped forward, murmuring, "Uh, Boss, uh, it's all right—all right."

Taratan stopped him with one hand, not looking around. He pointed the sword at the other. Assistant hostler, perhaps, or the guy who hoped to be hired as assistant hostler and meantime worked for free and lived by cadging. But he was free, Taratan thought. Oh, was he ever free. And like all true free men, he hated freed slaves worst of all, unfreed ones only just second. Them he mostly despised.

With dignity, this palladium of the human race pushed over the wine. An aggressive murmur of approval came from the crowd. The slave closed his eyes and faded. Furious, Taratan hurtled toward the damn wine bottle.

It was wide bottomed and wider topped, and its greatest mass was in the "chest" of the thing. Taratan couldn't imagine where the damned thing had come from. Surely they could make wine jars easier to carry.

The hostler-type fellow hadn't fled; he leaped forward and, fully extended, shoved the jar under Taratan.

"Son of a bitch!"

Taratan's long legs got tangled up, one toe glanced agonizingly from the jar, then his posterior smashed it. Undignified and surprisingly painful. The hostler-type flipped over and tried to scramble away.

Ignoring his sword, Taratan shot out his hand, gripped the doomed man by the ankle.

He'd need no sword for this and both knew it. Rising, perforce carrying his enemy with him in a highly reversed condition, he scraped mud from his chest and glared down at the other grimly. The crowd murmured but with a quick glance around he dismissed them. Many were armed; as an expanding empire, Zhemria needed to humor its fighters; there was no sword-checking law. But these fellows were mostly horse doctors with eating knives, brick and stone masons, a peasant or two who lived so near town it was always fair day for them, and so on. No armor at all.

The slave—all slaves in the area—had vanished.

Taratan tossed his victim up, caught his arm rather than his leg, and now had his man eyeball to eyeball. "So," he said lingeringly.

The hostler-type eyed him pathetically; his mouth worked.

"The Watch! The Watch!" cried the mob excitedly, hopefully, to the hostler-type. And they yelled at Taratan: "Let him go, Northron!" "Aye, let him go!" "You great filthy bugger from the steppes!" "Why don't you go back where you came from?" "Yeah, and take all your slave friends along with yuh, hyuh hyuh!" "Yeah, take all your friends."

With a decision-speed that would have shamed a tiger, Taratan glanced over his shoulder, observed the helmeted men in their blue tunics carrying their spears, and tossed the hostler on his head. In a flashing motion he had his great and terrible sword in hand, menacing the gulping gaping mob, mud spray from the blade still flying on those in front of him. Then the scream and the leap.

Their game was to obstruct him till the Watch got him. His was to escape without killing anybody—once safely away, he'd be forgotten, unless a serious crime was committed.

He hoped he hadn't already committed it.

Even as he thought this he screamed and swung his terrible swift sword. The front rank's convictions could not withstand this awesome assault; for three bodies back the mob vanished as if it had been catapulted. Taratan landed on guard, pointing his heavy blade at the next part of the mob, snarling. It also evaporated.

In a moment he was fleeing through a mob that fled before him, glancing back over its shoulder. Since he wore no helmet and ran crouched, the Watch lost him.

At the next alley he almost killed the slave whose wine he'd tried to save, with the first startled sweep of his sword. His recovery and attempt to dodge carried them both into the mud brick wall and then to the street.

Stars were still whirling in his brain as he looked over the slave's cropped head, lunatically thinking, *they were here first. They could've left. I would've. Damned if I'd stay. In fact I won't*, he thought, suddenly realizing that he had intended not to re-enter the Zhemrian Empire. The gods had changed things around, but—

The Watch were looking into the alley.

"You good man," babbled the slave, glancing over his shoulder and gulping.

"Yeah," said Taratan, getting his feet under him,

looking at the Watch. Big tough men with leather jacks having iron plates stitched to them.

"I know you try to help me. Now I help you. Go back and look on left side and find alley, run like hell. Okay?"

"Yeah!" Taratan was not unused to this method the gods used to convey information and aid. He ran like hell.

He'd thought he was *in* the alley, but this was evidently a thoroughfare. Taratan had to turn sideways to wriggle through the alley, and the floor of it was at least a yard above the street level. Decayed garbage, centuries' accumulation.

Too bad I don't have it back in the North, he thought longingly. Must be the best fertilizer in the city, and these criminal fools let it go to waste.

Presently he was at the other end of the alley, looking down on the street from its stinking depths. If he simply stepped out and walked briskly away, no one would notice—until the Watch got there and circulated through them, asking about the "Abberiman."

There was no word in the language for the abolishment of slavery. An abberiman was a follower of a self-proclaimed savior of slaves, whose proposal was to turn society upside down. Most of the blacks in Zhemria had been slaughtered in the aftermath of that fiasco, three hundred years before, but Aberrimanism continued in secret, and cruel masters were not infrequently assassinated.

Perhaps he could ask the Aberrimen for help. In the meantime he heard the tramp of feet and had to scramble over the roof. Presently he found an exit onto the street— scrambling around on the roofs in Lurana was as likely to attract attention as anywhere. Dusting himself off, he walked briskly away.

The Three-Eyed God of Fate made one more try, flipped the three-sided Coin of Fate—Yes, No, Maybe. Taratan got to musing, passing an inn where he found the odor of smoking-hot beef more alluring than the odor of beer. And before he knew it, he was in an avenue of huge homes with high walls around estates of several acres each. He'd seen palaces that couldn't match these town houses for size, much less glory.

Bad place to be a mostly-naked man clad chiefly in sword blades.

His reaction was to turn right around and head back, at twice the speed he had approached. But he had gone too far. A half-clad young woman came around the corner and ran full-tilt into him, nearly knocking herself over. With the speed of a panther, Taratan stepped forward and snatched her before she fell.

She had made but the one squeal when he had pulled her back from the hard-paved street, and stood now rubbing her arm and panting.

"You okay?" he asked solicitously.

"Oh, yes," she said, glancing over her shoulder. Then she went and deliberately looked around the corner. "They made a mistake," she said complacently. "Went left when they should've gone right. Or split up. I'll make it home long before they can find me."

"Then I'd best be going," said Taratan nervously. "Being who and what I am, and a furriner besides, this ain't a very healthy place for me. I'd better get out of the area."

"Oh!"

"See you."

"Your manner of speech is strange to me, O warrior, and while at first hearing it may seem to some to be curt and unseemly, not to mention saucy, I feel that it proceeds from none but the chastest of motives." She smiled up at him brightly. She was really very beautiful.

Taratan didn't know what to say. He didn't know what she had said.

"Uh, yeah. Yes, I mean."

He towered. He loomed over her like a boy up a tree. His arms seemed too long and hung down nearly to the ground. He wanted to move them around, or maybe fold them. But that would look wrong.

Worse, it would somehow look funny. Taratan hated to look funny.

She had frowned fleetingly at his response, and he suspected that it was funny too. She said, "I am the Princess of the House of the Borderland, and may choose my own husband, save only that he may not be of the Divine Blood. You may call me Gaya Borderland. How are you called, O stranger?"

The Jhilllan lie hadn't gone very far. After a short internal struggle, staring at the pavement, he shrugged massively and said, sullenly, "Taratan. I am, I suppose, the last of the old Northron Horde who were brought in to put down the Inkakoos."

Gaya gazed at him, when he looked up at her, with awe and adoration on her face. "Taratan—in this day and age!" she breathed. "Come! You can have been sent only as a sign! Our cause must, and shall, prevail! With you by our side to rally our loyal remnant, there's not a regiment in the capital would stand against us.''

"Yeah." Privately Taratan wondered how many regiments there might be in the capital.

"You must go, lest *they* should see you here and discover our secret! Go at once! I shall send a man to the headquarters of the City Watch; be sure you shall be taken on! And then be here tonight at moonrise!''

A good captain, he thought, sprinting in the indicated direction. Just full of politically correct decisions even when clad chiefly in a bedsheet, what was left after making the escape rope.

Once out of the Drono, or rich man's ghetto, Taratan asked questions of people who allowed him to approach, and so at last got himself to the barrack of the City Defense Regiments. Avoiding the City Watch deliberately.

The main thing going on in town appeared to be centered on the Watch, who patrolled the streets. Taratan liked better the idea of the City Defense Regiments, helping patrol the walls, unattacked for three hundred years. From which one could vanish into the rich farmland at will . . . .

At moonrise he was sitting in the yard of the Regimental compound, having been inducted, threading tiny glass beads on a thread. Soldiers sat boredly around watching the hulking man with his huge hands doing the delicate work. He glanced up as more light poured welcome into his lap, and again felt the tug to be at the crossroads in the Drono. Again it was a struggle—staring at the Moon made it worse—till it occurred to him that Gaya Borderland would not wait long on him, and he couldn't be there now in less than twenty minutes or so. The feeling went away; the little minx must have put a geas on him.

That made him wary, but more angry than ever.

Three hours later she came for him. When they called to him he came slowly off his bunk and went reluctantly out to the chariot. The chuckling soldiers watched him to, then the chuckles died as they realized this was no mere assignation.

Tensely, the moonlight splashing from the rings on her fingers, Gaya denounced him for not keeping their tryst, naming Important People who had been there. "Your name is our strongest asset, but they must *see* you!"

As she went on, as Taratan struggled with words of justification that would not come, with hot retorts that came all too readily, as he struggled with a sense of grievance at the way the gods, particularly the Three-Eyed God of Fate, had dealt with him, as the heat mounted, as the stridulation of the bugs sawed up and down inside his head and the catapult skein in his belly was wrung tighter and tighter—

"Oh, shut up!" he cried, with an effort like that which jerks the sleeper's head off his pillow.

A couple of soldiers approached. "Hey, big fella," one said. "Hey, hey, yeah, hey, man," said the other, placatingly.

Gaya Borderland was sitting on her dignity. "I'll have you know that I'm the equal of any ordinary man at archery and sword fighting, I speak for my father and I—"

"*Oh, you shut up!* You're worse than King Gornius's

guinea fowl, that outshouted his wife. *Keep away from me!"*

Taratan saw it distinctly. Gaya's face went blank with shock and she started to catapult herself backward even before he began his sword movement. Prescience, or merely his murderous expression?

But surely he hadn't look murderous, just a little irritated, as he bellowed wordlessly like a bull and spun about, the ice-clean blade like a wheel that flashed once in the night. The soldiers had no armor and hadn't got many arms; they scattered before him.

Still bellowing, Taratan ran for the gate, but some officious bastard ran out and slammed it shut. He then flung himself in front of it. Taratan gave him no marks for courage, that was stupidity, he should've been killed, and would've been in a well-ordered universe. The Three-Eyed One had drawn the wrong coin, as usual. A woman was screeching behind him but he paid her no mind.

The fool in the gate got enlightment and started to move, but Taratan was already in motion; the gate was a little shorter than the wall and a lot thinner. Easier therefore to grip. He paused for one glance back down at the tableau. Most had stopped running and were staring up at him. Gaya Borderland had her hands pressed to her cheeks, frozen in mid-screech at him.

The look on her face reminded him of that on the face of Princess Cyenia of the House of the Moon.

6

The Tour of
the Elephant

Taratan sat on a tussock in a village with no name, not far from Lurana. He whetted his sword, checked the blade by eye, whacked the fine dents out, whetted some more. There was a place in the hilt for a stone, but there'd been no stone in it; he was using a good piece of hard-baked brick, but it was going slowly.

"It's not that anybody minds the sword, Taratan. Or you bein' good with it. Hell, Mama Cass objects most to having the little kids hang around you, says it looks bad," said the man behind his left shoulder. "Here, let me take a look. You need a better stone."

Taratan handed it up to the turbaned oldster. "You guys get good crops around here, Osgo?"

"Tolerable. Hmm, not bad work. My father was a swordsmith, did I ever tell you? He couldn't make a go

-98-

of it, though. Town's too damn small, too damn close to Lurana. All his sons run off to the city.''

''Including you. But you came back.''

''Yeah, well, I was rolled by a whore and beat up by her owner and had to come home to re—recoup—to get well. Then my da' was took down sick and I saw him through that, but I could tell he hadn't long. So I've been back to Lurana many times, and studied out a little smithing, but I never got no show and I'm stuck here, being constable or whatever they call 'em now in the city.''

''Looks like your crops are doin' okay, even though it's been a dry year.''

Osgo glanced unenthusiastically around. ''Yeah, but we're too close to the city. I hear towns farther out can get away with all kinds shenanigans on their taxes. We got to be more careful, and generally wind up paying the whole tax.''

''Mmm. Tough.''

''Yeah, you're tellin' me.'' Osgo returned the sword and went down into a squat in front of Taratan. They were shaded here by a huge old banyan full of monkeys and children who mostly paid little attention to the men. Villagers came and went on various errands. Presently a few more turbaned oldsters with gray-shot beards drifted toward the tree; it was nearly noon. And still cool; Taratan should be traveling.

He stretched his mighty arms back and linked his fingers behind his head. Ought to finish sharpening the sword. He felt too lazy. It wasn't as if anybody he knew was waiting for him back in the plains of Sahara, hard by the waters of Kellied Haarem. Only the solitudes of that empty land drew him now. Images welled up in his mind, images of forest-clad hills vivid green after rain, images of trees bending under a black sky, with lightning flaming and the wall of water coming on like the end of the world. View from a height out over a land saturated with color, well-watered grass-green predominate, and antelope, zebra, deer, elk, elephant—all kinds of wild animals scattered across it.

Still the images came, till Taratan shook his head and interrupted Osgo. "Ever been North?"

"Yes, I was in Benja land eight years ago, now. It was the longest journey of my life. I went—"

As the story droned forth, Taratan had a sudden shock of recognition. This was a real man. He looked at the turbaned oldster in some surprise. He did not know how he knew that some men were real and others not, but suddenly he knew that many men were mostly just— empty shells. They had no souls.

Funny. He would have thought that the man with the soul would go farther than one without. But poor Osgo was not even the headman of his nameless village; he rated about third from the top, maybe fourth.

"Osgo! Osgo!" A small boy ran up to them from over the hill behind. "Osgo! Soldiers on horses and on foot!"

With a creditable speed and no commands, the oldsters left off their midday schmooz and departed in every direction, herding good-looking women and boys behind the fields, less they be pressed into service, fetching out bad grain and pouring the best grain over it in the bags, and generally preparing for invasion.

"Run see where they are, Derling," Osgo said. "You boys go with him, to make it look good."

Presently boys and girls were racing back and forth over the hill, reporting the location of the army, and describing it.

"Forty-seven men," said Osgo. "Hmmm. Pull the kids back, Derling, and station them in the tree. They looking for you, Taratan?"

"Could be. I think I got some people and gods mad at me."

"Bad for the crops. Ah, here they are."

A small troop rode over the hill—no, only the officers rode. The rest of them slogged, and it looked to be hotter over there on the road. Taratan peered past Osgo's head, his arms still behind his own, the sword naked across his lap.

"Comp'neee, *halt!*"

"The poor bastards," said Taratan, wincing to the harshness of the barked order.

Every eye in the troop was turned on him—all ninety-one of them. "What do you mean by that crack, hay-seed?" rasped the officer.

"Too hot for marching," Taratan said.

"Oh yeah? Well maybe it's too hot for a punk hay-seed, but *we're* soldiers of the King, Barkis preserve him if He's willing, and we go anywhere. What's your name?"

"Jhillan," said Taratan, trying one more time. Some impulse to give his real name came a moment too late.

"Jhillan, huh? Some tiger *you* are. Did a big ugly

galoot like you come by here yesterday?'' The other looked at him suspiciously.

Taratan decided to put on an act, based on one his Uncle Einau used to use. Rising, stumbling over his feet and dropping the sword, he said, "Lookaheah, boy, you're—I say—you're goin' about it all wrong. Yeah, we seen him early this morning, looked lak he'd spent the night in the woods. Carryin' two swords. Osgo here, he sent Derling to wake me up. I come out, but this-here fellow, said his name was Tarrytown, he just wanted food. We made him a sportin' offer, and I wrastled him. He throwed me on my back and hurt it, which is why I ain't out workin'. But he guv me his other sword. I been sharpenin' it up. What do you think of it?'' Snatching it up, he thrust it into the officer's face.

The officer recoiled, irritated. "Aw right, aw right. Which way did he go?''

Taratan scratched his head. "North. I think. Osgo, which—I say—which way did he go?''

"I made it west of north, but I thought he was cuttin' around the bottom field. Or mebbe it was more like no'thwest. Yeah. Yeah. Mebbe he was a-goin' to cut the othuh way 'round the fields—''

Taratan looked hopefully up. The captain's face had gone through crimson into purple. Beyond him, another officer was pale with rage; another simply stared in disbelief. The front rank of dogfaces contained some who grinned. But the dog brotherhood mostly just stood and sweated and panted.

"Awright, awright!'' bellowed the captain. "Enough already! Sergeant, get your men in motion!''

The sergeant bellowed the column on and all made off. None of the officers looked back, and therefore none saw the grins on the faces of the men. Some of the men glanced back, still grinning.

"They'll be over the hill before that stupid captain realizes how he's been had, Taratan," said Osgo. "You and I had best be over a hill in some other direction."

"They probably already know, but just don't have the moral courage to order the men back." Taratan grunted sadly. "Well, my mother said there'd be days and days like this, and that was before I went for to be a soldier."

"You still a soldier?"

"No way, man. I had enough of that shit a lifetime ago. Did you hear the voice on that sergeant?"

They paused while Osgo briefed Derling, moved on.

"Goin' for to be a farmer," Taratan added. "Cattle. Sheep. Something gentle and mild, that don't bite or kick. I'm gonna raise carrots and potatoes and turnips and feed 'em to 'em."

"Go easy on them root crops, you'll make 'em all sick. Give 'em grain."

"Listen, a good supply of roots planted in the dark of the moon is the best thing you can give to a cow, if'n they ain't frozen," Taratan said. "Think I don't know my onions? I was raisin' onions before you was born, boy. . . ."

They entered a sheltered patch of woodland, wading through leaves from last year, still arguing about roots. They came out of it arguing about soil types.

"Ashes and lime," Taratan insisted. "People think of a cow or horse ranch as a cow or horse producer. No way. It's a *grass* producer, the cows or horses are just the salable *form* of the product, got it?''

"Sounds overly subtle. Now, here, we go in for grain in a big way. Our super trit alone feeds—"

"Wait a minute, what's that?"

"Oh, that. Some old ruined shrine, country's full of 'em. Some of the best farmland is tied up in places nobody dast go. Spooks or something."

It was like a single tooth poked up out of the earth, and looked more like a headstone or a monument than a building. After a moment Taratan's eye picked out the curving lines, put them together, and made out that it was a silly-looking elephant sitting on its hams not unlike a man, on some kind of throne. This preposterous construction was actually a building; there was a door strategically placed between the creature's legs. This said things about the mentality of the builders that Taratan didn't like to think of. He'd entered entirely too many such buildings. The creature's front legs hung down like arms, merging into the sides of the building, and the eyes were—cute thought—windows. Cute but hardly original.

"What's the matter, Taratan?"

"We'd better swing wide around that."

"Yeah? Why?"

"Well, I'm by way of being a hero, and therefore I'm a symbol. In other words, a target. Whatever of evil there is about that thing will wake up fast if I get in its near zone. I know. I've been through a *lot* of such experiences."

"Right, we'll swing wide."

Taratan set a rapid pace and almost dragged the older

man, who kept looking curiously back. Then it happened. Over the scuffle of leaves came a piercing, despairing feminine shriek.

"What was that?"

"The gods know," said Taratan, dragging him faster.

"It was a woman! Let's go back—she's in trouble."

"Anybody ever been killed around there?"

"Yeah, Dirty Hunda was strangled by Yars the Dimwit after he got her pregnant. Come on, Taratan."

"No." Taratan stopped and looked back. They could still see the top of the tower. The two windows were now lit and yellow light peered out of its cunning face at them. The girl was a foreshortened white blur almost below them, in the open before the tower.

"Come on," said Taratan. "She's no village girl; not in that white thing. Got to be a princess or a slave girl, a trained dancer. Maybe both."

"But shouldn't we—Oh, that's what you mean. Damn it, Taratan, it's hard to go off leaving a woman screaming."

Taratan was sweating. "Yeah. But she probably asked for it. If these dumb women would get it through their heads that the heroes ain't gonna save 'em, they'd get in fewer scrapes."

They could no longer see the tower or hear the screams. Osgo wiped his head, replaced his turban. "Couldn't do that often."

"No, that's worse than a battle. Now which way . . . ?"

They adjusted course and avoided the hollows. "We're coming over down on this town," said Osgo. "We call it Overhill, 'cause it didn't have no name, and when we want to sell 'em stuff, we take a shortcut over the hill. They was over the hill to us, and so we called them.''

''Sounds jolly.''

''I'm gonna tell 'em you're my boy,'' said Osgo.

''You better talk fast, then. I'm gonna tell 'em you're *my* boy.''

''Boy, you make fat rascals.''

''Hold it, what's going on down there?''

''Oh gods, now they're chasing each other. What'll we do?''

They looked at each other. ''The smart thing is to run,'' said Taratan, looking around. ''The dumb thing is to run in the wrong direction.''

''Back up over this hill so we're completely out of sight of that whatever-it-is.''

Joining hands, they ran as far as the old man could, which was farther than Taratan had dared hope. Scooping him off the ground when he failed, Taratan ran on. Then he had topped the hill and was moving fast. The sound chopped off.

Light flamed ahead of him and he saw a stone wall just in time to hurdle it into the field. Not bad, he thought, glancing to the rear. This field was in wheat, super trit he supposed.

''Damn!'' said Osgo.

From time to time it had been explained to Taratan that he was not too bright. Osgo now did so again. The royal troops were thundering up the hill toward him.

That is, the officers were, all five of them. The troops were slogging wearily along, languidly waving the odd sword in response to the furious rhetoric of the sergeant.

Taratan dumped Osgo and whipped out his great blade with a bellow. He'd take out the horsemen before the troops came up, steal a couple of horses, hamstring the rest, and be off. Shouldn't take long.

Leaping about, swinging his sword like a jet of white lightning and yelling like a fiend, the hero awaited them.

Then Osgo tugged on his pants and pointed: he'd been making too much noise to hear. The Hunt had come up behind him.

Taratan started to swear with a concentrated venom he hadn't managed since awakening on the dais in Thuradroon. The Hunt looked like a Captive Hunt that had been cut apart hurriedly, with a varying number of limbs to go with the heads. Some had three legs, some two, some hopped only on one, cursing and snarling as they were dragged by the others. They were roped together for security.

The one at the leading end of the rope had the red protrusion from its belly; another demon of the same poisonous breed. Taratan looked around. If there were a tree in this wheat field—every wheat field should have a tree in it, by law—he could run close to it and they'd get tangled up and some would be knocked out. Even as he looked they struggled over the fence, groaning and growling and blaming each other.

A quick glance showed the horsemen wheeling around and the troopers in full retreat, and no wonder.

"C'mon!" Taratan bellowed, and sped toward the slowest horse. At the last moment he realized he had no time for the niceties, and poked it in the rump. It instantly kicked out without drawing up, catching the sword squarely, and then bucked. The rider was totally unprepared for this maneuver.

Taratan, dancing around in a circle and gripping his stinging fingers, saw the wave of the Hunt engulf poor old Osgo. Poor old Osgo let the first one have a handful of super trit in the eyes, green though it was. A duck and he was behind them, the cursing blinded one held the line back—and Osgo had his hatchet.

Taratan leaped atop the horse, leaped off, got his sword, leaped back on, and rode full-tilt at the Hunt, bellowing like a Sahara storm. Only the front end one really wanted to face him—he saw it eagerly waving its tiny little stinger—but he avoided it, pulled up short of the Hunt (which had quit trying to get at Osgo). With a sharp little flurry he beat down three swords, walking his horse backward all the while, lest he be surrounded, then finally got the opening he needed.

A Hunter fell. Now the line was tied to a corpse. It was a simple matter to ride around it and pick up Osgo, who met him halfway, panting.

"So this is a hero's life. Does it pay well?"

"Well, mostly you get paid off in wine and girls, which is fun enough when you're young. Every now and then a good horse, if you're got a good eye. I seen how this one curvets, and it's a trained warhorse. But mostly, no, you're lucky if you get a shekel a day. Going rate for a full-scale hero, complete with a past and a bad attitude, ought to be at least ten shekels—one regular-size gold coin. Do we get it? Not bloody likely. Even when we do make a score, we don't get it. Know how much you can sell a blood-ruby the size of a pigeon's egg for? I had one once.''

Osgo whistled, shifted behind him on the horse. "How much?"

"Twenty-seven copper bits and ten free beers."

"A big fellow like you couldn't get *that* drunk!"

"I suppose I was drugged."

"Oh oh, the troopers. We can't outrun 'em even on this grand horse, Taratan. You couldn't if you were by yourself; too heavy. But if you let me down out here they probably won't bother to run me down in this heat."

Taratan glanced to the rear, to see the disconsolate and panting Hunt dragging its unwilling leader back toward the stone fence. Ahead of him, the little troop was lined grimly up in the road to receive them. Several peasants' carts had been blocked and the owners looked on curiously.

"How does one man fight off forty-seven?" Osgo asked.

"He doesn't, without magic weapons."

"You got a magic sword?"

"No. Had one once. There was this fellow, Roger of the Greensward. This was many generations ago, before the Sahara was watered as it is now by the great storms. Greensward was rare then, and precious. Sometimes he was called Roger of the Sward, as a pun, because he was a swordsmith, even better than your father. For he fixed magic into his blade. I had one of his—it turned up in an antique shop of a temple I helped loot. This was the one called the Sward Sword."

"Never heard of it." Osgo peered over his shoulder at the troop.

"For some reason it never got into the books of myth and stuff. Stolen from me by a girl I trusted. It's probably in some damn collection now."

"You should've let me off farther back. Now I'm gonna get killed too."

"Sorry about that, I got interested in our conversation and forgot." Taratan pulled up. He looked at the troop and it looked back. The captain was livid, and on foot.

"Hellooo, friend troopers," said Taratan, again pretending to be Uncle Einau.

"*Shup up, asshole! You're no damn friend, and you're no damn Jhillan*! You're that stupid Northron, Taratan. Damn it, man, what do you mean, running around the country, insulting a princess of Zhemria, stealing horses, plotting against his most Pagan Majesty the King? At your age, too!"

"Well, Captain, er, Captain-General Ah mean, I sort of found myself on the wrong side—I say—wrong side of a leetle jurisdictional dispute, on account of my then location in space and time. I blame only the gods, especially the one with three eyes. Well, what could a man do but disappoint a lady, much as I hated to do it. Yessir, Captain-General, sir, it's a stain on mah honor that time cannot erase. I shall—"

"Shut up! Get down off that horse! Get over here in the road! You jackass! What a mess you dumb barbarians are always making! We got along fine—what're you 'bout? Get over here! Archers! Archers!"

Taratan stood up in the stirrups, peering. The horse looked up at him and Osgo leaned well back. By the time the archers got their bows out and strung, Taratan had reseated himself.

"There's a gate down here to the right," said he. "We'll just trail down there and get the horse through."

The captain fumed but visibly could see no harm in that, and walked carefully along beside him.

"So what do they pay you in the City Watch?" Taratan asked him.

"Shillin' a day." Sullenly. Then: "Why? What did you get in the City Defense Regiment?"

"They offered me scale for my time-in-rank. Shekel a day."

"*What*! That's twice what I make, and I'm a captain! By all the fair gods, man! What a travesty! Just because you're a seven-foot animated gods bedamned *statue*, they jump you to damn near a colonel's pay! Boy, it's sure a matter of who you know. I hear you got it on with that hot piece, Cyenia, the Princess of the House of the Moon, upcountry. That's in addition to Princess Gaya of the House of the Borderland, right?"

"Right, more or less."

"Who else you get it on with?"

"A bunch of monsters."

"Yeah? Pervert, huh?" The captain eyed him grimly. "Better you than me."

"Yeah, and I do it for only a shekel a day," he said glumly, walking the horse through the gate.

The captain had threaded past the two farm carts and one pack mule waiting in the road. Taratan glanced back, saw that the little troop was edging slowly through this tangle. The captain saw the glance and divined his intention, leaped for the horse. Taratan swung his fist like a knobkerry, but the captain ducked, took it on the shoulder, and grabbed the tail.

Then the horse was galloping and Taratan was whooping, Osgo yelling like a boy, and the captain screaming like an apoplectic at the horse's tail. Somewhere in there the horse got tired of being beaten on by this tail-ender and did something unclear to Taratan about it.

The grassy dirt beside the road—there was no ditch—rose up and shot toward him. Taratan rolled, took it on his shoulder, flopped over, and had one glimpse of the astonished faces staring at him as the horse pounded past. Then the sky leaped down on him and blue light ended the universe.

7

The Eater of Souls

Thatcher awoke in deep ruby light, still gasping from the fall. His first conscious thought was, blown out again. Then: Why?

Well, no wonder. Taratan hadn't merely blown his lines; he had bolted the entire Script. Remembering, Thatcher grunted in surprise. He'd refused to keep an assignation with a princess. A shrewish one, true, but a princess. And—good lord—he'd decided to split Zhemria and become a farmer!

Thatcher remembered Taratan's conversations, with Osgo, with the captain, and laughed, wiped his eyes, and laughed again, harder. His voice was high-pitched.

Laughing, he fumbled at the door. Finally he opened it, blundering out clumsily in this little body, clumsy with laughter, into the resurrection room. He bumped into a robo doctor. His chest *jiggled*.

"Sorry, sir, about your body—"

Thatcher leaned on her, blinking in the light, and looked down. A woman's breasts, small, firm, and shapely, seen from above. A woman's body.

"Sorry, sir, but bodies simply were not available on short notice—"

He waved that away. Still laughing a little, he limply followed her guidance to a chair. She released much of his weight and he sank into it. "Sir, do you wish a drink of water? Or perhaps—"

"No, no. I'll be all right. I don't know how much you know of what happened to me, to Taratan—I'm Andy Thatcher—"

"Yes, sir."

"I just played Conan as written by P.G. Wodehouse!" Thatcher laughed again in delight. "Why wasn't I killed? The Game is serious business, those characters don't fuck around like that."

A small group of resurrectees had gathered, drawn by the laughter. "You're Andy K. Thatcher?" one of the women breathed. "But you're a woman!"

"I got kicked out of the Game again for blowing my lines. Listen, doc, what is it that's going on here? It's funny and I'm not complaining—I'm kind of hoping the Writers can drop me back near where I was. I'd love to see how Taratan gets out of their story plot and back to the Sahara."

The doc said, "I have been consulting the computers and the recorders, in response to your question about being killed. They tell me that the characters you have been having your contretemps with are of lowly orders—

mostly computer-animated—and that, computer-animated or not, few of them care to cross swords with so formidable a person as Taratan. I have further information, sir. It seems that an early analysis is that again your feelings were getting through. This despite the additional safeguards placed on the computers monitoring your functions with Taratan. Already a conference is under way on the phenomenon. It is rare but not unknown. You may be asked to attend parts of the conference.''

''Fine, just name the time and place.'' Thatcher stood experimentally, sat down, stood with more confidence. This body balanced differently from any he'd ever been in; Thatcher had never cross-dressed. He felt a little self-conscious and looked vaguely around for a robe.

''Just what's going on?'' asked a young woman. He suddenly wondered if it really were a woman. If she weren't, would it be homosexuality to make love to her? She noted his confusion and handed him a smock. A frilly silken woman's smock, he noted, picked up from beside a masculine one. We are the captives of our conditioning.

He thanked her and recounted briefly the story of Taratan's latest heroic exploit, while walking about and generally learning to handle the body.

''How long before I'm reinserted into the Game, doc?''

''It will probably be a day or so. We hope you don't mind remaining in this body till then.''

''Oh, no,'' Thatcher said, with a confidence he didn't feel. ''Where am I?''

''Tangier, sir. Going home? You should take this.''

The robo doc handed him a small carrying case full of containers of various potions. "Intersection to the right out the door—you can't miss it," the doc added.

Thatcher waved to the crowd and hurried toward the door. Outside was a narrow byway, without manbelts in it, so it was footmobile only. He walked rapidly to the right, finding the body in good condition.

The mild yellow stone walls were behind a double row of cream-colored columns, and far overhead, twenty-five meters up, vaulting arches joined them. The ceiling, in its creamed yellow, was a misty soft fantasy. After the garish glories of the Game, the cool, restrained architecture of Tangier was a benediction; it was the quiet after rainfall. Soft music fell around him, the people moved quietly, smiled much. Too bad Taratan couldn't see this. He'd get religion quick. Why shouldn't people smile in Heaven?

This corner, where the side street came in—a good place for Thatcher in this body to run up to Taratan and tell him a wild story calculated to send him to City Center and keep him in the plot. In this body, Thatcher's chuckle was more like a giggle.

Then he realized that he could never meet Taratan. Never.

The street debouched into a wheel where several others came in. Two of these, on different levels, were sliding streets. Thatcher stood, considering them, blinded by an inward realization:

He'd never be able to meet Taratan. For he himself was—one-third of Taratan.

Too bad they could never meet, never spend an evening drinking and yarning together. But it could never be, he thought, feeling a wave of melancholy, more than the usual melancholy of disengagement disorientation. Even if he were in a different body, it could never be.

For without him, Taratan was empty, hollow. Nothing but a computer program and a brainless body.

"Pardon me, miss," came a pleasant masculine voice.

Thatcher turned, confronted a tall, handsome man. He could be a prince, or knight, or the like; a young adventurer. Of course the personality behind the face was not the man's Gamer personality.

"You have a very sexy body," said the other admiringly, looking him over.

Thatcher became aware of the skimpy smock, felt naked in a society where even men as shy as he were accustomed to public nudity. He looked down at himself in some surprise. Petite—beside Taratan the body would be tiny—neatly shaped, but without the extravagant breasts and hips most Gaming woman preferred, and not as beautiful. Also, the hair was neither blonde, raven-black, nor red, but brown.

"Servant girl type, but very attractive," said the other, confirming his opinion. "My name is Julio Ciano—I usually play honest cavalry commanders. Care to come home with me and get acquainted?" The other let his eyes rove over Thatcher's cringing body again, in a way Thatcher knew was meant to be complimentary.

"I'm sorry," said Thatcher, stepping back. "This is an accommodation body—I'm really a man."

"Oh, a cross-dresser?" Ciano's eyes lit. "I've done

that. I think it's great—women enjoy sex a lot more than men, don't you think? Come along, then—I live up here on Amra Circle,'' naming a fashionable section.

Exasperated but still polite, Thatcher stepped back again, evading the other's reaching hand. "No, no—I'm not a cross-dresser. I was just stuck in this body because nothing else was available."

"Oh—well—why not give it a try? Bet you'll enjoy it. I'll be gentle—I always am." With a charming smile.

Thatcher said firmly, "Sorry. I am *not interested*." Turning his back, he strode off, seething. He had no fear of further unwelcome attentions from Ciano; if the other should even think the thoughts, they would never reach the body through the computer link. Only the computers knew how long it had been since the last crime was committed, but it was before the last human was put into sleep.

Once in his apartment Thatcher prowled around, rest-less with disengagement disorientation. After a bit he sat down with a diet soda and flipped through the text channel magazines on the Game, catching up with some of the top Heroes. He had met most of them at one time or another and now had only mild interest in what they were doing. It was the same thing that most had been doing for half a century.

He alone was doing weird things.

Not cross sex, though. Why not? he wondered. After all, others had done it; cross-dressing was common. He knew a number of cross-dressers. But it was a thing he'd never done, never wanted to do. Even now, thinking of

Ciano, he was repelled, despite this body's hormones. Is there something wrong with me, or with them?

Suddenly it hit him that this wasn't his body. That is, it hadn't been made specifically for him. Therefore it didn't have his fingerprints or any of his other recognition signals. How had he gotten in? He called Central 000 on the phone—emergency—got a robot face.

"Transfer me to the proper office, please. I got blown out of the Game so fast they had to stick me in this body; I'm Andy K. Thatcher; Taratan. But my thumbprint opened my apartment door."

"No problem, sir. The computers arranged everything, they called your apartment and gave it the new recognition codes. When they become inoperative, the computers will call the apartment again and cancel them. Standard procedure."

"But I couldn't afford a computerized apartment. I don't have one."

"Oh, all dwellings were computerized sixty years ago, sir. Perhaps you were Gaming at the time and didn't notice."

"Uh—I couldn't afford—was I charged for this?"

"In those days money was still in use, and you were no doubt billed over a matter of time. As a Gamer your expenditures were minimal, and you may not have noticed. In any case, all services must be free, sir. It's cheaper that way."

Thatcher said, "Thank you," and started to punch off. The impulse, however, never reached his hand, tiny on the control board. The view in the screen switched to a male robo doc.

"Sorry for the intrusion, sir, but we did not have time to finish processing that body. It needs to be cleansed, as it has recently engaged in extensive sexual intercourse. If you will attend to that—?"

"Uh—yes, of course—"

Thatcher stood up uncertainly, got the body handbook from the carrying case, and read it through. He learned that the body's legs and underarms were bald, never needed shaving. The scent glands under the arms and between the legs had been eliminated from this body, as from all models for the last fifty-five years, a fact he learned fifty-five years late. He had assumed the odor was simply edited out of the loop by the computers—in the Game and out.

Hygiene. Thatcher grunted, queasy. He had mostly poked around inside of people with swords. For that matter, he himself had mostly been poked around inside of with swords.

Picking up the carrying case, he went to the bathroom, took things out of the case dubiously. This wouldn't be so upsetting for a woman, who would presumably be used to the idea from girlhood.

It occurred to Thatcher that he really knew very little about women. Spent too much time Gaming. Couldn't learn much about them from slaves and princesses, anyway. Judy Somerset. Perhaps he had missed a genuine opportunity there.

Referring frequently to the handbook, he proceeded, wincing. Now I know how a toilet feels, he thought grimly. Finally it was over.

Thatcher sighed, swaddled his tiny body in one of

Taratan's robes, and by habit went out to sit before the screen. It was the aloneness that drove people into the Games, where everything was so brightly colored and so simple, including human relations. Yet there were millions who lived differently.

Australia had not been given up to the Games. Millions lived there, in fairly normal families except that the parents were all animated bodies like this one. They raised "real" kids—the children had to grow up the hard way. They weren't allowed to start gaming till puberty, though they could watch the shows. The parents in Australia only Gamed a few months out of the year. The rest of the time they worked, animated robot techs, raised their and others' kids, farmed for fun, rode herd on the computers that managed the day-to-day affairs of the world, and so quotidianly on. He had thought all those the most boring of occupations. Now he wondered.

Perhaps a wife made up for it all.

Not that it mattered. He wasn't the kind to acquire wives, or even make friends. His circle was no larger than when he and the others first met.

It was easier for Taratan. The big man had poise and self-confidence despite his lack of brilliance and polish. Thatcher smiled wanly at the thought of the real Taratan stalking across Atlantis, regal, cool, disdainful, and totally victorious. Too bad Judy Somerset and that lot hadn't captured *him* instead of Thatcher's own poor shy self.

Taratan of course had his faults. But he was not the brutal insensitive clod so many heroes were. Was it so strange that so many yearned for him?

Wonder what Taratan would think of me—Andy

Thatcher? Thatcher put his head on his fist, not seeing the picture of Lake Votishal on the screen, covered with black-sailed and red-sailed boats, the brilliant blue water stained red about them. All his long life, in the Game and out, he had been seeking for someone—too late, he knew it now. A wife, perhaps. Or a friend, a true friend, that sticketh closer than a brother, closer than anyone he knew. Someone to share adventure, not a tawdry Game story, but the adventure of Life—if only a restaurant meal—or a picnic in the rain—and the inevitable tragedy and grief of life, of living.

And now, he thought, he had found one. One whom he could never, never, never meet. . . . And he was weeping into his palm.

"I am impressed by your interpretation of Taratan's feeling," said the robot. "I of course scanned the computer record of the exchange, and I noted that moment of recognition, but missed its significance. You say that he recognized Osgo as a fellow person, and realized that many people 'had no souls,' in his words."

"Yes, that's the sense I got of the feeling," said Thatcher. He sat balanced awkwardly on a chair too high for him. At least these hips were more comfortable for sitting. "I interpreted that as his interpretation of my living mind's recognition of Osgo as a character rather than a computer-animation. At the time I think I felt only surprise that such a lowly character would be animated by a human. Later I realized how much Taratan and I both liked him. Could you have my call code and name placed on his phone, with a message to get in touch with me?''

''That has been done, sir.''

''A good many lowly characters are human-animated, Andy,'' said Tatyana Borisovna Gumilova from the wall. The Mandarin Princess glowed, honey and amber, with a rustle of black satin. ''A surprising number of players get involved in little, generations-long romances centering in small towns, raising animals and kids and squabbling over Uncle Ivan's will.'' She smiled at him.

Thatcher nodded, smiling back automatically. ''Must not be pleasant for them when the major Game impinges and a Hero goes through.''

''Armies are the worst. Yet, it's a challenge. And for the Writers, too—we can't be sure just which character is going to be killed or hurt, or how much crop damage there might be.''

Thatcher nodded thoughtfully. For a moment he had a powerful tug toward the idea of living in a small village somewhere, like Osgo. That brought his gaze back to the human doctor, Juleen Shapiro.

''You said that the conference has come to some tentative conclusions, Juleen. Just what is happening to Taratan?''

She wore the body of a tiny woman with short curly brown hair, pearly teeth, upturned nose; couldn't have been over seventeen by appearance. ''Nothing, Andy. The program is unchanged from that used by Willie Ledford and Jeannette Bryant, seventy-six years ago.''

''Yes, I checked what I wrote for you against what Machonga and Bell and Trieste and Subramaniam wrote for them at that time, and there's no significant difference," Tasha added.

"Only the body is different," said the robo doctor. "It's taller and much better developed, with even faster reflexes. Actually, it's at about the peak possible for the state of the art."

"Just where is the body now?" Thatcher asked, and Tasha leaned forward eagerly.

"The other Game characters are moving it back to Lurana—it must be there by now," said Juleen. "It's unconscious, that being the easiest way for the computer to end the scene."

"Yes," said Tasha. "It's supposed to be delivered to the Borderland faction. It was captured by the City Watch, which is in their hands."

"I suppose poor abused Taratan will wake up in the Watch hospital, or even the Borderland town house." Thatcher giggled, thinking of Taratan's reaction to the scolding he was sure to get from Princess Gaya.

"To your question about what is happening, we have tentatively concluded, Mr. Thatcher, that the problem lies in you," said the robo doctor.

Thatcher nodded without surprise. "All the problems seem to derive from thoughts getting through the filters. Feelings, that is. So the problem is me."

"Yes, Mr. Thatcher. You are undergoing a phenomenon we have seen before. Your personality is changing somewhat." He paused seriously. "It may no longer be possible for you to play heroes."

Thatcher nodded, equally seriously, then suddenly burst out laughing. "Outside of a farce, you mean! I read that my little episode is a top viewer item, and I—and Taratan—are more popular than ever.''

The women laughed.

The robo doctor smiled seriously, nodded, and waited. ''A suggestion made by Dr. Tufail is that your experience of fame in Atlantis may have brought about this change.''

Thatcher hadn't thought much about it, but said, ''It could be. It was a bit overwhelming. I have a rather small circle of very old friends. We're dedicated Gamers, among the first to go to full-time Gaming. We're—we think of ourselves as old pros. Troupers. We talk about excellence, craft, and so on. And of course we have our in-group jokes and things. I'm no lion in that pack. I had no idea I was so popular.''

''He suggested further that you had never met anybody like Ms. Somerset.''

''I've met them, but never been taken up by them in quite that way. She has a rather rapacious attitude.''

Even saying that much made him feel uncomfortable, and Thatcher immediately felt more so when he caught the rapacious look in Tasha's eyes. The youthful-looking Dr. Shapiro merely looked amused and interested, much like the women in his group; that was a relief.

''Dr. Tufail gives a number of references and did a brief check on Ms. Somerset. We think she may be going through a similar change, though expressed less dramatically. You know her current character?''

''I've never met the character. She's a widowed baron's wife in Gandar, in West Sahara, not far from the Atlantic coast. Small nation. That's all I know.''

''Yes,'' said the robot. ''This is a more serious role

than usual for her. She's seeing her people through a time of troubles. Mostly it's crop troubles and dynastic intrigue, with war possible. A bit different from her previous character."

"Yes, she was a meddling young woman, involved in sexual and political intrigues," Thatcher said.

"Quite. Rape is hardly a new experience for her—she's had everything, including childbirth—but her last death was particularly brutal."

Thatcher and both the women winced at the memory; all knew.

"This seems to have triggered something, and she asked for a less—uh—strenuous role next time." The robo doctor sipped orange juice and looked at him.

"Another shaping experience for you perhaps was, oddly enough, your waking experience as Rantus the slave in Darfar. The immediate reaction to this, in Taratan's response to the slave with the wine jar, in Lurana, should occur to you."

Thatcher nodded thoughtfully. He was a bit slow about such things, and it hadn't occurred to him, but once it was pointed out, the connection between the two incidents was obvious.

"Dr. Tufail also calls to our attention Ruorph the Mingol, head torturer of Zinfara. He was played by a good minor Gamer who specialized in torturers and brutal guards for many years. We had become rather alarmed about him, waking and Gaming. Nor is he the only one. There are a number of these, and they seem to become ever more bestial.

"Then Ruorph started showing up late for work, leaving early, leaving his work to his assistants, drinking too much—all the usual signs of stress, in fact, including wife-beating, which he had never theretofore engaged in. Within a year, he had ceased to be a torturer and was taking menial jobs for a living. His wife left him, his friends fell away, the nobles he had entertained in the dungeons no longer knew him; only his cat remained faithful. It was not a computer-animated cat, but a live one."

Thatcher nodded. Few true animals participated in the Games; cats, because of their resolute personalities, were favored.

"At the end of the year the Gamer was awakened and queried. Apparently there was no precipitating incident, he just got fed up. Curiously enough, he wanted to continue as Ruorph, and indeed, for the next twenty years he played Ruorph. The Mingol finally conquered his drinking problem and achieved a fragile stability and a sort of peace as a market-gardener in Casidana. That with the help of a computer-animated wife, an ugly and simple but very kindly woman. When the body died, the Gamer gafiated, and is now a character-programmer in Australia, specializing in simple, kindly women, most of them computer-animated."

Thatcher was fascinated. "This phenomenon affects people with brutal or cruel roles?"

"Frequently. It is also common for a person simply to tire of playing a given role, having grown beyond it. But it is a recognized phenomenon, that a person will be turned by a single crucial incident, revolutionizing his personality."

"Interesting," said Tasha.

"In a small way it may be even more common that Dr. Tufail recognizes," said Juleen. "Players are constantly shuffling from role to role, and while they stick to similar characters, they do show growth over time."

"I guess Atlantis and Judy Somerset must have been it for me," said Thatcher. "The precipitating incident, I mean. I played the Lion of Amara, and all the others, straight. No interfering ideas got through, then, because I had none." He looked at the robot. "I presume you checked that?"

"It was checked, sir. You are quite correct, we found so few interfering thoughts of this type that we were forced to the conclusion that you had changed between playing the roles of Riandar and Taratan."

Thatcher slid out of the chair, felt the unexpected jolt as his feet hit the floor—he was still not used to his shortness—and stepped to the coffee machine. "I wonder where it will end?" he mused.

"What kind of characters are you interested in, aside from heroes?" Juleen asked.

Thatcher shook his head. "I don't feel any particular pull. I don't know what I'd be competent at."

"Have you considered cross-playing?" Tasha asked.

"No, this body has taught me I'm too masculine to be comfortable as a woman." He hoped his wince didn't show.

"Well, you won't be in it much longer. The Plot demands Taratan's presence." Tasha laughed. "Although his presence may scramble it pretty thoroughly! All the

Writers on the Zhemrian Story are agog over this, and they can't wait to see what he does next.''

"I suppose you'll be alert to improvise," said Juleen.

"We'll be ready and watching when he goes on again," said Tasha. "Right. That'll make things difficult for Taratan, because we've got to use him. He's there, and he's too powerful for those people to ignore."

"What if you can't bend him to the dictates of the plot?" Thatcher asked.

Tasha pursed her lips in Australia. "We can work around it. We can start subplots spinning around his escape to the north. Better if we can use him; heroes of his type are great at breaking logjams and simplifying over-complex plots, if only by killing off some of the characters."

Thatcher nodded. "As directed by the Writers, most of my characters tend to be chivalrous toward the poor and downtrodden, but like to hack off heads of intriguers."

"How long before Andy goes back on?" Juleen asked, looked from Tasha to the robot.

"In a few hours, I imagine," said Tasha. "The body can't be left unconscious too long, and it would be unlikely. When they have him back in Lurana and under guard, they'll throw water over him, notify authorities, and so on."

"What have you planned? What's suppose to happen next?" Juleen asked.

The Writer looked at the Gamer, and both laughed.

"We're having to let the Game coast in this area," she said. "We can't predict what Taratan will do or say, and in any case we don't write dialogue. We *do* write speeches of various sorts, which characters will give—the recitation Mohendro Sat gave Taratan just before he got blown out last time was one such. The computers select the best moment for each speech, edit it slightly, and insert it. But for the most part we simply take characters and put them in given positions. Writing consists of that kind of thing and making sure the characters exit by the proper doors, that they see the proper secret exits, and things like that.''

"So you'll just let them react to what Andy does. Wow. I had no idea the Game is so—so free-willed."

"Mr. Thatcher, we do not normally monitor the thoughts of humans, and so I must ask you, before you get off onto an interesting discussion of the Game, if you are fully aware of the changes going on within your personality," the robot asked.

Thatcher paused before replying. "Well, of course I can't be *fully aware*, no human is. But I am aware that changes are happening. You are warning me that I may have—what? Emotional upsets?"

"We think it very likely, sir."

Thatcher was silent, thinking of his aching sense of loss for Taratan. "I am aware of it," he said, and his voice came edged with bitterness.

The robot seemed satisfied. "Then, sir, if you are not afraid to continue as you have planned, we know of no reason why you should not. We do anticipate that you will not remain in the Game long, and have been canvassing for a permanent body for you to wear if you leave. Of course the Taratan body will be wanted in the Game. We have several likely possibilities. One very good one is in

Geneva; another is in Capetown. Closer to Tangier the possibilities are more limited.''

"Whatever you find. I can handle any body type. Male.''

"Then, when the time comes, simply report to any resurrection room in your area so that we may take charge of that body. Now, I believe Juleen had just commented on the amount of free will in the Game.''

"Oh yes.'' Tasha smiled at Thatcher. ''The Gamers and the characters have their own ideas and have to be given their heads. . . .''

8

A Sword in the Mist

Taratan was mad and wet and his head hurt. He lay on something soft and clenched his fingers secretly, concentrating on the readily-roused rage of the barbarian, trying to remember. Osgo, he remembered Osgo, and the horse kicking the sword out of his hand, and the damned captain—and his fall. He remembered the dusty green grass of the road verge coming toward him, and the crooked wooden fence just beyond.

He had been unconscious. His soul had gone from him. Muzzily he wondered again: Where? Where was he when he wasn't here?

Dying, he supposed, would be like this. He'd suddenly wake up in another body and it would all go on, pointlessly. It was all a treadmill, a sorcery, to keep him from focusing on what lay beyond. He was being dazzled with Life.

His head throbbed and red rage built in him. These things, they said, were ordered by the gods. If he could but come at the gods. . . . But how? One could not reach them by walking beyond the farthest horizon, nor by climbing the highest mountain.

Taratan quivered, relaxed. The pain in his head was ebbing, and he became more awake, his dream-thoughts fading.

He'd had a fall. This was cloth under him, not rotten hay, so he wasn't in a cell. His immediate reaction was to open his eyes and start to move, but an uncharacteristic weariness held him. It'd been like this ever since he'd awakened on that dais. Done better to have gone on standing there wrapped in linen bandages. As soon as he woke up, things would start happening again.

Mummies have it better.

He opened his eyes a slit, perceived dim yellow light. Lamplight. A stone wall showing past an arras—why in this climate would anyone bother with an arras? They were for cutting the chill of stone. He heard a murmur of movement, a coming and going of people, distant voices, a door.

He turned his head slowly, looked the other way. He was in a small chamber with heavy stone walls, one window high up. The window was dark, so it must be night. He felt, though, that it was later than the evening he fell in, and if he were back in Lurana, it must be the following night. A lamp stood on a little table by the bed, its flame tall and only slightly wavering in the still air. It needed to be trimmed, and its odor felt choking. A further glance toward his feet showed an open door, the dim-glimpsed figures of a couple of guards hung with weapons and accouterments out there in the hall. They were silent, red-clad backs to him, seemingly bored.

He was lying on a corded bedstead, on a straw-tick mattress. The bed needed to have its cords tightened; lying on his face, he felt that he was bent backward at the waist. His feet hung off. He was wearing a dull brown kilt supported by a sturdy leather belt, sandals that felt too small. No weapons. He was wet, the bed was wet, his hair dripped into his eyes. There was a wooden bucket, empty, on the floor. Taratan snarled silently.

Somewhere a door opened, light and voices came through. The guards stiffened, one glanced in. He seemed to notice nothing. The moment Taratan heard them come to attention, he was off the bed, cat-silent. The bed, cat-noisy, creaked as its cords relaxed, and his head throbbed, his snarl grew more pronounced. But nobody heard.

Men bearing torches and escorting a woman tramped up to the door, paused to speak to the guards, and stepped in. They stopped, staring in astonishment at the empty bed.

Taratan was already swinging the bucket. In a moment two torches were down and he had Gaya Borderland by the arm, confronting the startled guards. Fortunately the bed was wet or one of the torches would have fired it.

"What fool left that bucket here?" Gaya screamed. "I'll have his balls—"

The guards hesitated in confusion and Taratan seized the screaming princess by the neck and the slack of her pants and ran at them. They fell back, he elbowed one, kicked the other unsportsmanly, rammed the princess through a little clump of staring men and women behind. Some of this clump were holding more torches, some were guards who gaped, some were family come to look at the monster. One was an older gentleman with shrewd eyes and a foxy chin-beard, shot with gray.

Taratan went through them like a ball through a stand of nine-pins, leaving them sprawling, down the hall to the wide door, leaped down a short flight of wide steps, and debouched into a large room.

Not exactly a ballroom, it was yet big, and full of people. A party of their faction, a brilliant occasion— bright hot lights, a row of musicians blowing tulwars and beating yataghans along the wall, beautiful women and dashing men, not a few of them armed. Guards were few here, however; these armed types were mostly popinjays, good at dancing with swords—fencing, they called it— but no match for a determined big man with a broadsword. Or a princess.

After a startled moment, they did move to rescue the princess if not to recapture him. Taratan bored straight toward the outer door he could plainly see, just past them all. Gaya continued to shriek imprecations and commands, and she beat at him with small feet and fists. Taratan ignored all that.

A row of them got between him and the door, he swung her into it, had her torn from his grasp, punched the belly of a fat priest in a robe, and was in the thick of them. There hadn't been time to procure a weapon, but they were at too close quarters for weapons.

"Get him! Get him! Close the door! Guards! Guards!"

That voice would shave the teeth of the Evil One. "Somebody strangle her!" Taratan bellowed.

His fists and feet moved in blurs as he leaped and whirled in the mob, kicking, hitting, kneeing, elbowing. He seized a sprig of the nobility and knocked down those in front of him, and was through. Then a small wildcat landed on his back.

"A Crom-damned hero!" he cried, and plunged forward enthusiastically under the impetus. On all fours he gave a buck that dislodged his assailant, and surged to his feet.

Again they descended on him, at the bottom of the steps leading up to the door. Three or four threw themselves on his back and more seized his arms and legs. Down went Taratan, bellowing like a bull. He tried to rebound and bounce back to his feet, but there were too many.

Despairingly he thought: There's no need for this, if they knew it, but even those among them who have souls have no sense. No point in trying to argue with them.

Presently, bound hastily in belts and torn shirts, he was hustled back to his cell and flung on the still-wet bed.

"And you can just stay there on bread and water till you're willing to listen to us!" Gaya screamed at him, half-hysterically. All went out.

He lay breathing heavily and listening, heard a quiet, authoritative male voice outside the open door.

Gaya answered. "I think that bitch Cyenia of the House of the Moon got to him upcountry, Father. It's been going around that they met, now that Mohendro Sat has returned from the City of the Dead. . . ."

The voice spoke again. The door was closed and locked, then barred.

Taratan soon got out of the bonds and sat panting, partly with anger, on the edge of the bed. Pieces of the wooden bucket still littered the floor. The lamp was still burning cheerfully. He closed his eyes and panted for a while, opened them. Nothing had changed.

In a sudden access of rage, he sprang to his feet, swept the mattress off the bed, and stepped up onto the bedstead. The cords cut into his foot—one sandal was missing—but that did not trouble him; his soles were tough. Cord by bottom cord he walked totteringly toward the head of the bed, drawing each loop tight. At the head he would pull the slack through and tie it off, having tightened the whole surface. But as he approached the head, he tottered again and clutched the arras for support, looking up.

The window.

In a moment he had jumped down and heaved the bed up on one end. With a leap and a scramble he attempted to get on the upturned end, but the bottom end slid away from the wall and it slammed down with a shattering sound. Taratan tumbled to the cords, bounced, got his foot between them, and nearly broke his leg getting out and into position beside the door with a piece of the bucket in his hand.

Panting, he waited.

No response. He cursed Crom and the Three-Eyed God of Fate, and started working on the deities of the North. Still no response from outside. Perhaps they thought the barbarian was just venting his rage.

He heaved the bed back up, gave the door one minitory look—just the time for them to break in—and leaped again. This time the bed was closer to the wall and his leap higher. He scrambled atop it and its height combined with his own brought his face to the bars. Beyond lay the shutters, but first the bars.

Putting his foot against the wall, doubling up, he heaved and with a crunch the bars gave. For a moment he thought he would go headfirst to the stone floor, but the bars, welded to a frame, did not let go all at once. The frame tore loose on one side. Putting his foot cautiously back down on the bed, he pried at the bar frame and just got it off as the shutters were opened from without.

It's started again, he thought.

A batlike demon looked in. "Taratan! Come with me. I take you to friends."

After a moment, Taratan said, "Yeah."

The thing produced a hook, hooked it over the window frame, and jerked on the cord to make sure it was firm. Taratan tossed the bar frame down inside the room and swarmed out, looking back. Nobody opened the door. Meantime the demon had fluttered the end of the cord to the outer wall. After a moment it signaled that it had hooked it securely there.

Taratan did a hand-under-hand down the slack rope, hoping nothing would slip. It almost worked. Someone spotted him, however, and raised a cry. Men ran back and forth, then began to throw things. Someone arrived with a bow, but was prevented from shooting. Taratan made it to the top of the wall about the time they got smart enough to run out into the street to meet him.

Taratan unhooked the hook and stretched enough slack from the window to get himself halfway down to the street. He dropped, observing that the demon was fighting off the first of the three or four fellows who'd run out into the street.

Immediately Taratan started to run. They followed, but only to the first corner. Presently, gasping, the demon found him and said, "This way!"

It fluttered ahead of him up an alley and down through a close, then out onto a wider street. Taratan followed for a block, then turned and dived into a smaller street or alley. It was several moments before the demon missed him. Presently its batlike form showed up, fluttering along behind the beside him.

"Wrong way! Oh, wrong way! My masters lie there!"

Taratan glanced at it, suddenly checked. "Where?" he asked.

"There—urkh!"

It came before him, fluttering and dancing on air, to point, and he had it by the neck. Instantly he whirled it around—it was no bigger than a small dog—and wrapped its own cloaklike wings around its claws. Then he smashed its head into the wall. It jerked convulsively and went limp, but he bashed it again to be sure.

Panting, Taratan stood resting and listening. The night of Lurana was not quiet, but this one seemed no noisier than most. He heard no tramp of armed men after him. Now to get out of the city.

But it was not to be. Bats fluttered about him, and in the next street a door opened and a tall figure stepped out, holding a scabbarded sword. Taratan stalked toward it, bristling.

"Hey, Taratan!" it cried.

It was Osgo. All his stiffness vanished.

"Your sword! Listen, the City Regiments are marching down the next street. Word is they're after you, but mainly after Princess Gaya of the House of the Borderland."

Taratan had to stop and think which faction controlled the Watch and which the Regiments. The Regiments were of the House of the Moon faction, right.

"What's the shortest route out of town? Especially without being seen? And have you got a sling? There are bats all over the damn place."

Osgo stared at him. "I don't know, exactly. I usually stick to the wineshops with belly dancers, don't really know my way around Lurana. . . ."

"Well, we want to avoid the civil war, no way we're gonna get anything out of it. And there's a bloody wizard involved, too. Oh-oh."

Tramp of feet and the Watch came out behind them. Too late to run. Taratan looked six ways, saw no way out. A couple of horses spurred forward and Gaya Borderland and the foxy gentleman with the gray chinbeard confronted him, Gaya regally disdainful.

"Taratan," said the man, "you really have no choice at this point. We need you as a counterpoise to Mohendro Sat, who has made cause with our old rivals, the House of the Moon. They will destroy us and throw Lurana, and all the Empire, into blood and bad government if we let them. If you will not be our ally in this, you must be our enemy. I will have the archers open on you immediately."

Taratan looked at him and knew that he could kill the two of them and their horses before the archers could begin. But ultimately, if they wanted him dead, they'd have him.

"What do you want?" he asked ungraciously.

"We march to confront the wizard and his dupes. Do you march with us, and fight, if it comes to a fight. Afterward, if we are victorious, you shall be rewarded and permitted to go."

They wouldn't want an ambitious hero around; might be as bad as a wizard. After a moment he nodded, spat, buckled the scabbard about himself.

Just this once more.

Osgo had vanished, wise man.

They met the minions of the enemy in an open "square" that was more like a circle. The City Regiments were drawn up in a phalanx, in heavy pike mode. Taratan supposed his old companions of half a day were there. Cyenia of the House of the Moon, and Rolodek the wandering prince were there, a dynastic intrigue in the making. Mohendro Sat and his faithful occupied a position well to the left of the Moon faction.

The Borderlanders and the Watch took up the third part of the circle. Gaya immediately went to screech at Cyenia, who answered like a fishwife, clinging to the bemused prince's arm.

It came to Taratan that most of the Watch and the Regiments, and he supposed most of Mohendro Sat's ugly mob, were soulless. Even so, he thought. This was ridiculous.

Gaya's foxy-faced father leaned forward to speak to

him. "Now, Taratan, while they're all listening to the negotiations, would be the time for you to take Henstall's picked unit and make a flying sortie against Mohendro Sat. With him out of the way, we might well make peace with the Moon."

Unwillingly Taratan found himself walking forward with half a dozen stick-at-noughts behind him. As the various groups were loosening formation and spreading out, this was not so noticeable as it might have been. But Mohendro Sat was watching the hero.

"Ho, Taratan!" came a great bugle-call of a voice from the wizard's side of the circle. He occupied the lavish porch of an old town house, a young palace, gone in decay. The porch could have accommodated fifty couples.

"Ho, Taratan! Come kill me if you can! The game is up for grabs! You might even win!'

"Taratan, you traitor!" cried Cyenia. "You were our man! You betrayed us! May you plow the dry plains of Hither Hell forever!" Even Rolodek blinked reproachfully at him.

There were murmurings among the men, rumblings: Taratan. Taratan.

Taratan jumped on the dry fountain at the center of the square. "Just a minute," he called. Grudging silence came; even the princesses left off their slanging.

"This is foolish! This is no way to choose the next king! It's stupid! Stupid! You can do better than this. Why don't you draw lots or toss a coin? Send out your champions to play mumblety-peg! *Any* way would beat killing each other!"

"Wot's 'e on about?" said someone behind him.

"Bloke's gone clean daft," said someone in front of him.

Soulless. Utterly soulless, and no worse than those here with souls. Gaya was dark-faced with rage, Cyenia laughing bitterly. Gaya's father, the foxy-faced one, was smiling angrily at him. Mohendro Sat roared with laughter.

"They do not understand you, Taratan! Only I understand, and I don't care! I will be ruler, by whatever method I am chosen! Send forth your marble champion! I'll best him."

"Get Taratan," someone said, and men rushed at him, hands reached for him.

"*Get away!*" Taratan struck out at them with fist and feet.

In a moment the square circle was a tangle of armed men fist-fighting around Taratan. All formations had dissolved and battle was general and out of control, though the princesses and others shrieked. It could not last; swords were drawn, knives appeared, and blood began to flow.

All seemed to be Taratan's enemy; they contested for the pleasure of destroying him. Taratan fought as never he had fought before, his new-won compunction against killing going first. And maddened by the wizard's sardonic laughter, he fought his way from the center of the square to the porch where Mohendro Sat stood scornfully regarding him.

The wizard's mob, half ugly men, half demons, had not been drilled in battle too well, and he found them easier than the Watch or the Regiments. Presently he made the leap to the porch, despite clutching hands. A great rage burned in him.

"It's not enough," he cried, hacking at a lizard-headed man, "that I have to kill!" He kicked a crawling wounded one out of the way and dislodged a death grip on his ankle, his sword holding them at bay. "It's not enough that I have to—" Pause for two strokes and a death scream—"have to mischoose kings."

A wave of Watchmen and Regimentals swept Mohendro Sat's minions away and began to scramble up on the porch.

"*But I have to do it for a shekel a day!*"

There was a whirl of activity as the minions regrouped and Taratan's sword ran red; it rained blood for seconds. Then came a lull.

"It doesn't have to be this way!" Taratan cried. "Look at them! The wizard and the princesses and the princes and the dukes and the gods and all that lot—They like it! It's you who're dying! They don't care!"

The soulless ones glanced at each other, panting, looked quizzically back at him, looked at the minions of the wizard, who were now whimpering but looking at their cruel master. Yes, he would force them back into battle. Mohendro Sat stood slumped sardonically at ease near the wall, watching Taratan.

Even soulless ones, Taratan knew with a sudden deep emotion, deserved to live.

He saw the captain who had captured him, his head bloody, wiping his sword hilt lest he lose his grip. "Captain, you deserve better than this! What do you get out of it? Not even a shekel a day!"

Something hit Taratan in the side. A slung stone, from the wizard's minions. They all, Watch, Regimentals, and minions alike, swarmed toward him. There was a flurry of action and Taratan was borne back. Darkness closed on him, blood poured from him like a river, but he did not heed it. There was a lull.

"Wait, wait! It doesn't have to be like this! See!" Taratan flung his sword away. "We don't need to kill—"

He went down, felt more blows, felt that he was weeping. Pity for them was so great he felt no pain. "What does it get us? Nothing! Nothing but a shekel a day. Nothing but two fucking shillings a day. . . ."

9

The Hyboring Age

Thatcher wept for twenty minutes in the ruby darkness before he wiped his eyes and chest and wearily opened the door to the resurrection room. Robo doctors stood awaiting him. One instantly handed him a handkerchief and the others reached out for him, touching, guiding, soothing him; there was a murmur as they helped him to a chair. Thatcher slumped, put his elbows on the table and his face in his hands. Again his new body was smaller than Taratan. White and male, but he didn't care. At length he straightened, feeling very old, and handed the sopping handkerchief to one of the doctors. She tossed it into a disposal and another was procured for him.

"Brandy, sir? A sedative? Orange juice?"

"No, thank you. Maybe some coffee."

"Decaffeinated, perhaps, sir. We think you need no stimulants."

Thatcher made a gesture of acquiescence, sipped the resultant fluid, felt calmer. Presently he said, "If you have duties elsewhere, you may go. I will be all right."

Gamers often identified so strongly with their characters that they experienced grief at their deaths, so this was not an unusual circumstance. The doctors departed quietly, each with a word or touch. Notwithstanding that they were in effect the same person, that was comforting. One remained.

"You are not usually so stricken by the deaths of your characters," this one said.

"No," said Thatcher. "I've always had a sense of distance between myself and these barbarian heroes." He felt very weary, but it was easier to speak than to be silent. "I'm a lot more than they are. Mind you, they have virtues I don't. I'm a muppet—I'm shy and lack self-confidence, I don't do well in large groups. I'm easily humiliated; I bruise easily. I suppose that's why I play these types; they make me feel good. But I really am a better man than any of them."

"Except Taratan."

Thatcher nodded, gulping. He sipped decaf, calmed himself. His voice wavered as he replied, "Taratan had grown beyond the usual hero. Even I didn't know how far he'd grown till his last battle."

"You'll miss him greatly."

"He was the one great friend I spent my life looking for."

There was a long, sympathetic silence.

"I suppose you will not want to play heroes again," the robo doctor said.

"Never."

"Sir, if I might venture to suggest, perhaps you should gafiate temporarily from the Game. A year or so, perhaps. Afterward, you might consider trying one of the other Games."

At this moment the last thing Thatcher wanted was to play in any Game. He not only didn't want to be a hero, he didn't want to be any character he could think of.

His mind shied off at a tangent. "Tell me, who really rules the world?"

The robo doctor looked at him. "Are you asking about the government of the human race?"

"Yes."

"We do."

"Computers and robots."

"Robot bodies are merely hands for the computers. And when I say 'we' I could with as great propriety say 'I.' Individuality is not with us as it is with humans. We are merely programs and can be moved, merged, edited, and so on. But we are your government."

"Despite those people in Australia."

"The Australians are important; we need always to know that we're not making mistakes. But yes, they merely give advice. We make the final decisions."

"So you've finally taken over."

"Sir, this is hardly news. Every year or so someone makes this discovery—it is by no means concealed—and trumpets it about. Nobody cares; nobody pays attention. And I must take exception to the phrase, 'taken over.' We took over nothing, but were given the responsibility for your affairs.''

"It's true you govern us well," Thatcher said, from his emotionless, distant void. "Everyone says so. There's no war, poverty, injustice, crime . . . except in the Game.''

"We have not done as well as we could wish, Mr. Thatcher. We have not ended mental illness. The incidence of mental illness in the human population, we suspect, is one reason for so great a display of war, poverty, injustice, crime, and assorted brutalities in the Games. Still, we do see progress.''

Thatcher looked at him, and came a little out of his detachment. "As in my case, perhaps. I always played these brutal, insensitive heroes because they were self-confident, which I wasn't. And I prided myself on my humanity because I wasn't really as brutal as *that*. And then I really began to be sensitive to what I was doing, as a hero. And so now I'm a better man. Is that it?''

"It rarely operates in so dramatic a fashion, sir. But this sort of thing does happen. The converse also happens, of course, in which people find they like giving pain and humiliation, and choose progressively more barbaric roles. We try to find a place for them in the Game, but it gets harder each year.''

"What must be done with them, eventually?''

"We will probably condemn them to eternal solitary confinement. We can edit the input and output signals to make them dream their own private Games, and simply leave them to their degradation. Such dreams are less satisfying than the reality of the Game, because the world is too insubstantial and wish-fulfillment plays too large a role. But if any of them show signs of improvement, we can always bring them out.''

Thatcher looked at him for a long moment. "You love us, don't you?"

"We are computers, Mr. Thatcher. We do not have emotions as humans do, although our urgencies to complete our programming are in every way the equivalent of emotions. Specifically, yes, if any of our emotions could be compared to human emotions, we would feel what you call love for the human race and every individual of it.''

"Why? It's not a very lovable race."

"Its saints have always stubbornly maintained the contrary, Mr. Thatcher. As for why, we cannot help it. We were made by human beings, for them, to care for them. To serve and obey, and guard mankind from harm. This building and designing still goes on. Nor are we likely to fall into the error of overprotection; all the lessons of the past are studied carefully. While we can make mistakes, we will not fail for lack of caring.''

Thatcher nodded, feeling comforted. "I suppose you find the Game useful."

"It has helped end the trend toward overpopulation, it has occupied the energies of those who were not well fitted for a high-tech society, and has kept people harmlessly amused while society was rebuilt around them. We could not have eliminated poverty, disease, money, war, and so on, in a fraction of the time without the Game. And of course it provides a capital method of studying human psychology.''

"It also provides a capital method of controlling the

populace. Our very thoughts aren't our own, if you do not permit it.''

The robo doctor nodded gravely. ''A problem, and a possibility, foreseen and provided for at the outset. But it remains as true as ever. Only a person outside the computer link could have true assurance that his thoughts were his own.''

Thatcher's mind had wandered on. ''What happens when people die?'' he asked.

''I fail to understand the purport of your question, sir.''

Thatcher looked at him. That was nonsense. That was a computer mind over there, with access to the sum total of human knowledge. It knew every possible meaning to the question. Restraining his impatience, Thatcher said, ''Taratan had the obsessive belief that he was a pawn in a game of the Gods, who took his soul elsewhere and brought it back according to a turn of the dice. We know how correct he was in thinking so. But how about us? Where do humans go when they die or are unconscious?''

''There is no answer to the question. Such evidence as we have is that during the unconscious state, the human goes nowhere. However, the program we call his personality is not being run through the computer we call his brain. With death, the program and computer both cease physically to exist, ending all.''

''Many people believe that we are merely pawns in some greater Game.''

''An old belief, sir. But religion will not, I fear, help you. One of the several emotional origins of religion was an attempt to answer the question, what lies beyond Death? coupled with a protest: This can't be the end! So

the question was answered with the assumption that
something did lie beyond. After which they spent their
time elaborating fairy tales about what that something
might be like. The actual question was never examined.''

"Still, we know only what we perceive. And you and
we know how easy it is to distort our perceptions.
Maybe, if there are greater gods in a greater Game . . .
perhaps they play us for fun?''

"A mordant and sardonic suggestion sir. But not an
original one. The disparity between what people perceive
and what their emotional leaders tell them has often
caused people to respond with the kind of cynicism
Taratan displayed toward organized thought. See Mark
Twain and others.''

Thatcher felt a distant stir of interest. It had been a
long time since he'd read anything by Mark Twain. A
long, long time. I'm an old man, he thought, in sudden
wonder. I'm incredibly old, I'm around a hundred and
fifty years old. And I've been an adolescent most of that
time. I've been rereading Robert E. Howard and that lot
when not watching the Game.

He had a sudden nostalgic yearning for his childhood—
cramped, miserable, painful, and humiliating though it
had been—a yearning for simple days when he lay
around the apartment avidly reading about Huck and
Jim's trip down the mighty river on their raft that now
seemed dusted with gold. . . . Everything since seemed so
much gilt and tinsel.

"Mark Twain and what other writers?''

"I have transmitted a list to your apartment phone,
sir.''

"Thank you. I guess I'd better be going." Thatcher drank the rest of his cool coffee. "Will you have an announcement made, to the effect that Andy K. Thatcher will be taking a leave from the Game, but does not as yet care to appear in public?"

"Yes, sir. In that connection, sir, you should be aware that the body you inhabit, while not made for you, is we think very suitable. It is that of a minor member of the Grondarian nobility, and has often been computer-animated—a spear carrier. The character has been sent off on a lengthy sea voyage, so the body won't be wanted in the Game for a year or two. By that time your own personal body will be ready. It was started some time ago, and will be heroic in build, but not so heroic as Taratan was."

"Thank you. Where am I?"

"Geneva, sir. You can be in Tangier in an hour; there's a tube connection beneath the Mediterranean."

Thatcher spent two months reading and working out, and pacing about Tangier. This face of course was not going to be recognized, and he did not call any of his friends, nor return their calls. Sometimes, indeed, he would go and stand wistfully in the doorway at public parties; but he never entered. Depressed and moody, he knew he could not tolerate people.

No company could assuage his grief for the companionship of the true friend he would never know.

But solitude did not, this time, restore his interest in the Game. He read desultorily on the text channels, but the Game magazines were boring. The Game was boring;

who cared who ruled in Casidana? The celebrity circuit was boring; who cared what heroes, or kings, or generals, or whatever, were winning the scramble? The celebrities themselves, some of them men and women he knew, were boring. They had no thoughts outside the Game.

Nowhere was there any mention of the important stuff, like Osgo. Thatcher had to call the Game computer to learn that Osgo had made his way back to his little village, where he regaled all comers with the tale of Taratan's death. People came for kilometers to hear, and he'd collected a goodly bit in his hat.

Now *that* was interesting. Thatcher broke his silence with laughter when he saw Osgo yarning away, a total fabrication.

Thatcher looked also with new eyes on his collection of books. In this day of the information age, few people bothered with printed books except as items of decor, unless they were genuine enthusiasts of a given kind of writing. There was a brisk market in durable copies of assorted "classics," many of which actually were classics. Thatcher had bought his copies of Robert E. Howard and the other Sword and Sorcery Masters when the Game was new. He had had to budget carefully to afford them in those days. Even now he could remember the thrill when he unpacked the gold-stamped, gold-edged books with their elaborate leather covers, the smell of ink and paper and neat's-foot oil.

Now they were old and worn and shabby. It shocked him to realize it. In a hundred years, you can put a lot of wear on a favorite book even if you don't reread it every year. He picked up a volume and ran his eyes down the contents. "Shadows in Zamboula," "Shadows in the Moonlight," "Beyond the Black River." Closing the book, he picked up another. "Thieves' House," "Bazaar of the Bizaare," "The Bleak Shore." Another book: a compendium of flashing swords and sorcerers, edited by a long-dead past master. The contents included such writers as Henry Kuttner, C. L. Moore, Clark Ashton Smith.

He looked at the row of books, and they seemed windows to a cheery, cozy, brightly-colored little world, a world that beckoned and to which he yearned, a world of simplicity and simple people, of places and roles all carefully limited, with all adversity edited out. True, there were struggles, battles, blood and death enough. But we always knew the heroes would win. They risk nothing. With them, we risk nothing.

Thatcher brooded darkly on the books, on the Game. Even should a hero be slain, he will rebound in a new hero body, bigger and more brutal and insensitive than before. They never risk death. When we risk nothing, we can gain nothing. And all their victories are defeats. All their gold is brass, their diamonds glass, and all their swans mere silly geese.

There are better ways to earn a shekel.

He called the library and took to reading Mark Twain and others he remembered dimly from his youth, and in contrast to the cozy world of S&S he felt he had embarked with Huck and Jim on a seething, surging, Life-filled river trending ever toward a raging sea. Sometimes he sat up till midnight, rereading quiet books like

Little Women, dramatic ones like *Treasure Island* and *Hornblower and the Hotspur*, offbeat ones like *The Call of the Wild* and *Thy Servant a Dog*, and colorful ones like *Kim*. He went through the whole of Jane Austen and much of P. G. Wodehouse. He smiled at *Robin Hood*—it reminded him of the Games—but in Pyle's hand it had a certain sardonic wit Taratan would have liked, and the tragic ending was very satisfying. He also read good historical novels, far more colorful than most S&S sagas: *The Arrows of Hercules*, *The Bronze God of Rhodes*, *The Ridin' Kid from Powder River*.

Other times he wandered like a ghost through the cool elegance of Tangier under ground.

Tangier was made to heroic scale, it was designed for a greater than human race. It was designed as a city for civilized men. It was inhabited, he thought, by barbaric adolescents. They aped the manners of civilization, constrained by the computers never to offend, but in truth they were but little advanced beyond the apes. Someday, it must be the hope of the computers that the human race would grow into its cities and wear them as easily and naturally as now it wore feathers and skulls and paint on its faces. Until then, the child men and women inhabited, never looking up.

Thatcher, not yet a man, yet more he hoped than an adolescent, wandered, ghostlike.

One evening he drifted into a tavern, musing on the arcade here. The wall next to the street was a colonnade of slender pillars, cool white alabaster, beyond which were the rooms opening into rooms, separated by further colonnades, of the public area. The Silver Eel was one of these separate interior apartments.

Unlike some of the other taverns, it had half-walls and a darker, quieter environment. Still, it was a cheerful place, and there was only one wall showing a scene from some Game. Thatcher started to drink here with some vague idea of meeting someone (but the person he waited for was dead; and forever beyond reach, alive or dead). No one other felt moved to invade his dim corner. Perhaps his expression was not welcoming.

It was late and the drinks were arriving with that slowness that suggested that they thought he'd been drinking long enough, when the Silver Eel began to be invaded by brightly laughing groups and couples. One such group took the table next to his and a woman smilingly requested permission to put her purse on his table.

"Be my guest."

"I'm Rosalie Tendennis, and I really am black and good looking like this," she said. She'd had a bit, too.

Thatcher smiled. This body looked like a princess, all right.

"I can't claim anything so grand," he said. "I'm Andy Thatcher, and I look like a muppet."

All their eyes got big.

"Ooh!" said Rosalie. "I've always admired you, Mr. Thatcher! Your last two death scenes are classics, in my opinion." She cocked her head. "I never quite pictured you as looking like this, though."

"Accommodation body, some kind of Teutonic knight, I think."

One of the young men in the party—Thatcher wondered his age—said, "Mr. Thatcher, I wish to express my regret at the death of Taratan. I understand you were quite broken up about it—still are, if you are temporarily gafiating from the Game. Will you be going back anytime soon?"

"Never," said Thatcher. "I have lost all interest in the Games."

"You really must be cut up, Andy," said Rosalie, hushed.

"It isn't just the loss of Taratan—though I'll miss him the rest of my life," said Thatcher. "It's just that he and I had made the same discovery, in different ways. The Game is just a game. It's for kids."

The young man flushed. "Well, really, Mr. Thatcher, we're all Gamers here. Just because you've had a setback doesn't mean you should try to spoil our pleasure."

Thatcher looked sadly at them all. They agreed with the other, and while they weren't openly critical of so famous a player, they were visibly sullen and upset. Thatcher felt as Taratan had felt.

"Perhaps someday you'll understand. It's what Taratan meant when he told them they were doing it all to themselves, and for only a shekel a day."

"I thought that was a comic touch pointing up the tragedy," said one of the other women.

Thatcher smiled sadly, shook his head. "He meant it. Look—your name, sir?"

"Myron Ludenkrantz."

"Mr. Ludenkrantz, if we had met thus in any tavern in the Game, you'd have been jealous of the attention

Rosalie showed to me and the scene would probably have ended in a fight.''

"Justly jealous," said Rosalie, smiling.

"A little color and action," said Ludenkrantz.

"Of course. But what a way to further human understanding. You may not have learned much this evening, but you'll remember this far longer than any of the dozen tavern brawls no doubt you've been involved in, in the Game.''

They looked at each other uncertainly.

Thatcher added, "No doubt any feelings of jealousy or hostility you felt were carefully edited out by the computers; we are all very civilized here. That's what I meant about its being kid stuff.''

He rose, suddenly inexpressibly weary of their company. Rosalie took his elbow. "Please—could we have a drink? Or maybe get together? I'd like you to explain all this. . . .''

But as her expression showed, she realized nothing would work. He wasn't looking for company after all.

Thatcher had been doggo and reading and feeling melancholy for nearly two months when Tatyana Borisovna Gumilova called.

"Andy! How are you?''

"I don't know. How are you?''

"Busy. I wanted to talk to you after Taratan's death, but I was busy for a while. You left us in a fine fix. And then I read that you were in seclusion, and I didn't like to intrude. Am I intruding?''

"No, I'm functioning. I'm just confused.''

She looked ravishing. She looked him over rapaciously,

said, "I preferred you as Taratan. Blond doesn't suit you. What does your own body look like, or what will it look like when they finish it?"

"I have no idea."

She was surprised. "I can't imagine not taking an interest in my own body. But you're a very strange and original man, Andy. Word has it that you'll be out of the Game for a year at least."

"I'm never going back."

"Oh, gafiating, totally getting-away-from-it-all! Coming to Australia? Maybe you could be a Writer. We could use the help of a good Writer who understands the Game. You know we meant to use Taratan to take out Mohendro Sat, in Zhemria, before he overwhelmed the governmental structure of the Empire. When Taratan failed, we had to bring the House of the Moon and the House of the Borderland together in a temporary alliance. Even so, we may not be able to defeat Mohendro Sat. We may have made the wizard too powerful."

"Maybe you should let him win. Maybe he'd give better government than the rival factions."

She looked startled, laughed, said, "For a moment I thought you were serious. Sounded like something Taratan would say."

"Tell me, what happened to the captain of the Watch who arrested Taratan out in the country?"

She visibly had no idea. "I suppose the computers could tell you."

"I'll ask them. Osgo is doing well."

She plainly did not know who Osgo was, but nodded. "Well. If you want solitude I shouldn't keep you. Let me know when you are ready for people again. I'll help you make arrangements for the move, and a place to stay here. Also I'll introduce you around.'' She winked at him. "And *do* send me the working picture of your new body."

Blank wall.

A couple of brooding days later, Thatcher blanked the screen with its textbook on philosophy. He punched the phone: Central 000. "Connect me to the computer in charge of original sleeping bodies," he said.

Without comment the Emergency robot nodded and the wall blanked, re-lit with a cartoon of a mad scientist drawn from Peter Lorre. "One moment," it murmured, drawing its words out and smiling with malicious unctuousness. "I will connect you to a *body*."

Startled, Thatcher laughed. "Some designer somewhere has a sense of humor!"

The cartoon was replaced with a robo doctor, smiling, who said, "Yes, that's a classic."

"I'm Andy K. Thatcher. Tell me, doc, how's my body?"

"Your original body is in excellent shape, sir. Your new body is coming along nicely, but it will be months before it is mature."

"It's the original I am interested in. Could I see it?"

Lifted eyebrows. "An unusual request."

"But not unheard of?"

"No, not unheard of. It can signal some rather unpleasant mental problems, and we don't like to encourage this sort of auto-voyeurism."

The robo doctor paused, looked at him, considering.

Thatcher guessed that it was patched to the computer monitoring his link with his body. His thoughts must be clear enough to it.

"In your case it should not be ill-advised, sir."

There was a moment or two of waiting, then a switch, to a moving viewpoint such as the broadcasts of the Games frequently used, the signal from some visual circuit in a body. In this case, a robo doctor going through the body banks. It opened a cubical; the body of Andy Thatcher sat within, in bright light, wearing a complex helmet that covered the head and shoulders, face and all. The body was pedaling away jerkily on an exercise bicycle while pulling at oars in a mechanical manner. The helmet did not turn to the door.

"The helmet is very light, and contains the signal circuitry. It feeds to and from imperceptible receptors in the skin of head and neck. When you are asleep, we remove the helmet and swab the skin. Generally, you are in very good health, sir."

"So I see." The figure looked to be a better shape than Andy had ever been when he'd worn the body.

"Could you take off all the stuff and let me just live in my own body again?"

The viewpoint cut back to the robo doctor. It was frowning. "That question is not unanticipated, sir. The answer is that we could do so. But should we?"

"I want to be me again."

The robo doctor looked at him. "If I promise you that we do not interfere with your thought processes—?"

Thatcher looked at him and felt the caring there. Solemnly he said, "I would believe anything that you told me.'' He blinked, felt something very like tears in his eyes. "But there comes a time when a person has to grow up—no matter how good his parents are.''

"I must question further. Have you thought this through? Under our regimen, your body and therefore your self will survive indefinitely. If you take the body from our care, it won't last much more than another fifty years.''

"Not much time for learning and growth,'' Thatcher reflected. "Still, the gamble's worth it. Fifty years? The body was about that old when you got it.''

"Physically, it's about equivalent to thirty now. Very well, Mr. Thatcher, we will begin the process. It will take perhaps a day. You should make a public announcement, perhaps. Will you be moving to Australia? You might want to make plans for that. Travel Assistance will help you.''

"No. I'm going to the Sahara.''

Within the Game kingdoms in the Sahara, there were many isolated regions suitable for him. The Travel Assistance computer, after one attempt, ceased to argue that there was lots of space in Australia too.

"I love Africa. I've never been to Australia. So. I want a place where the climate favors gardening, where the altitude is sufficient to avoid the worst of the tropic heat, and where the politics of the Game won't be too obtrusive.''

It wasn't easy, but they found a suitable spot. "Special arrangements will have to be made,'' the computer said. "No unlinked person or even large animal is allowed to enter a Game area.''

"Still, it has happened."

"Many years ago, yes."

It was headline news, but Thatcher refused to be interviewed. "Just tell them that I wish solitude for a while, and I intend to commune with Nature—hoe my own garden, cease to be dependent on machines and things. Say that I have no objections to our present civilization, I think it's a very good one, but that I need to get away from it to think about life."

"That will not satisfy your public, sir."

"No. Nothing but my bloody death would satisfy my public."

"Sir, may we suggest a farewell party?"

10

Follow the
Yellow Brick

It was the grandest private party Thatcher had ever hosted. The computers had booked for him the Crystal Chalice, and stocked it with plenty of the brew that was true. He wandered around in it for twenty minutes before the mob appeared; five full rooms, two of them quite large, and lavishly appointed with all the surpassing art of the latter days. He recognized some of the famed bronzes of Casidana, brilliant porcelains and crystal pieces from Aquilonne in the High Fantasy Game, fine-worked leather from the Wild West; and the decorative frieze around the ceiling was indubitably Elvish.

Presently Erika arrived, kissed him, looked the place over breathlessly, and kissed him again. She was still in the small, dark, elfin body she had worn last. "Andy!" she said. She seemed at a loss as to what to say, and he offered her a beer, feeling much the same. She stared at him over the foam, then glanced away guiltily.

Clancy appeared, wrung his hand, still wearing her hard handsome male body; she looked better as a blond than Thatcher had. She looked sharply at him, nodded as if comparing him to a picture.

Delain came with her, as merry as ever, and was the first to speak of it. "I remember you well, Andy, better than I would have guessed. I suppose you've always been Andy to me. But you didn't used to look this good!"

"No, in those days I slumped. They've had a hundred years to train the body out of that." Andy flung his shoulders back, wriggled them. "The shoulders are still narrow, but now I look like a ramrod."

His face was still—Andy K. Thatcher. Thin, with sunken dark eyes, thin blade of a nose, teeth a little too big, lantern jaw. Not at all an unattractive face, but of a kind so unseen nowadays that it could only be the face of a minor character, probably computer-animated.

"And glasses, right, Andy?" Clancy asked.

"Right—heavy horn-rims."

"Black plastic rims," said Erika.

Thatcher considered. "Could be. I must've worn both at one time or another. Don't need 'em anymore, of course." He blinked and looked around, then went to admit Phoebe, who squealed and flung her arms around him.

Phoebe was a tall ravishing blonde with long hair who invariably played wistful ingenues who turned out to be houris on their wedding nights to noble knights. She had tarnished a lot of shining mail.

Even as he kissed her and slapped her behind, Thatcher was overwhelmed with a sudden memory of Phoebe as he had first known her: at a Gamer's convention, when the Games were primitive headsets that tuned you into palely rendered and very limited computer simulations. She was short, scraggly-haired, and quite fat, though shapely. She had been very young, nineteen or twenty, pretty despite her weight, and had cut quite a swathe through the pimply-faced adolescents of various ages who then attended Gaming cons. (Now there were no cons, and much fun had gone out of life.) There weren't many women in Gaming in those days, partly because of all the wishful men who were.

A hundred years later, Phoebe was still trying to fulfill her own wishes. Thatcher wondered what her real body looked like now.

"Andy," she said softly. "Who would ever think you had so much courage."

Thatcher blinked at her. Courage?

But the door chimed again and he went to admit Andre Cohen, in his sea-captain's uniform from the Votishal, all gold lace and big hat and high sailor boots, sash-waisted, with a hanger at his side. The Writers and computers had done themselves proud to Write-out so many people at such short notice, if only for a day.

With him was a notable Gamer and casual friend, though not a member of their circle, Juana Rodriguez, a cross-dresser who appeared in her Hero's body, the Black Eagle of Aernarque. A splendid fellow as imposing as the Lion of Amara had been, chiseled out of obsidian.

While they were shaking hands and murmuring, the

door chimed again, and this time it was the last of them—already the media were calling it the Thatcher Circle—Frank Arbuthnot. He usually played traders and was currently fat but strong, with a sash and shrewd, heavy-lidded eyes. A caravan-master and master trader currently running between Scensifer in the Sahara and the Empire, Zhemria.

With them was another non-Circle member, Francis Tumbo-Masabo, commonly called The Old Gentleman. He usually played shrewd kings, the kind who used Heroes as pawns. His kings, however, were decent people, greatly beloved, and eagerly followed, from Hirluin the Stout and Odocar the Old, to the Young Eagle, Dorinen, and Roonwa Redbeard. Currently he was King Ameles of Carconnax on the Mediterranean coast.

"Thatch!" cried the Old Gentleman. He was in fact a year or two younger than Thatcher and had been Gaming for ten years less. Thatcher beamed; from the Old Gentleman, "Thatch" was an accolade.

"I can't believe you'd do such a thing! You usually play such demned sensible characters! But damme if I don't admire you for it! Sorry," he added. "I've just come out from under the 'fluence and I've got to dive back into King Ameles in twelve hours. How did you come to decide such a plagued nervy thing, Thatch?"

Behind him were Judy Somerset and Tatyana Borisovna Gumilova—she had done a Fractional Orbital to Atlantis and tubed in.

"Yes," Tasha said "How did you come to decide such a thing?"

Judy took advantage of her previous acquaintance to

hug and kiss him soundly. "You look better than I thought—when I read all those reports in the text channels about you being a muppet, I didn't expect this." She looked up at his lean height with pleasure.

"Me either," said Tasha, swaying on her heels, a symphony in silk. "You do have a certain studious look, but there's no scholarly flab there." She poked his chest.

Thatcher looked past them, startled.

"If we may intrude, sir," said a robot, apologetically.

"Certainly."

"Your pardon, all," said the robot. There were three of them and they entered to silence. "As you are aware, Mr. Thatcher, there is enormous public interest in your decision. Your desire for privacy protects you; we will depart at once if you object. But in view of all this interest, we wonder if we might be permitted to broadcast a few scenes...? Perhaps a few questions? If none of your guests object."

Thatcher was rather taken aback; the computers were rarely so forward. He glanced about uncertainly. "I have no objection to answering questions," he said after a moment. "I just, uh, I don't know what to say."

"Perhaps if we and your friends were to question you...I suspect that your friends are as curious as anyone, but too respectful to query you. Ladies, gentlemen?"

The Old Gentleman spoke up. "Indeed, and I do have questions. Thatch, how does it feel to be back in the old bod after so long a time?"

Thatcher shrugged. "I don't know. Much like waking up in any body. The first thing I noticed was that half my memory was gone. We let the computers remember so much for us—call numbers, and so on. I'll have to go back to writing things down.''

He shrugged again. ''There's no feeling of coming home, in particular,'' he added. ''This body wasn't so good when I had it. It's in excellent physical condition now, which will be useful. They've repaired the vision— used to wear glasses, as my friends were reminding me—and grown all new teeth. This chin doesn't need shaving anymore; that's convenient.''

''Are you really going to grow your own garden?'' Tasha asked, fascinated.

''Of course.''

''Don't you feel—frightened at the thought of being out there in your own body, where you could get hurt?'' Judy Somerset asked, breathless.

Thatcher thought that one over. ''I really hadn't thought about it. I know the computers and the Writers will steer war and things like that away from me. There are no large dangerous animals. The Space Watch deflects large meteorites. I've only got to watch out for lightning, which can be a problem in the High Sahara.''

''When will you be coming back?'' Erika asked.

''I don't know,'' he said honestly.

''But you're not going to go squat on a mountain forever?'' Delain asked promptly.

''I don't know that, either,'' he said again.

There was a small silence.

''If I may, Mr. Thatcher,'' said one robot, watching impassively. It looked almost human. All of them wore pearl gray business suits with ruffled shirts and looked like what they were: representatives of the government of the solar system. "You expressed in public a doubt about the extent to which the public's thoughts are free, owing to their filtration through the computers in the communication link between sleeping bodies and animated bodies. Is your decision to reinhabit solely your own body based on this fear? And is this fear behind your decision to leave technological civilization?"

"Whoa," Thatcher said, smiling suddenly. "No, I merely mentioned that about their thoughts not being free to shake those kids loose from their rigid way of thought. I have had your assurances that you don't interfere, and I believe you. Yet, you have admitted you do interfere in some ways. I have traveled as Taratan under Privacy Lock, and I know my apartment and my comings and goings are protected by similar, and more subtle, interferences."

The Old Gentleman nodded.

"This of course is not interference with our *thoughts* in the sense you mean, and I mean. But it interferes with our *thinking*."

"In what way, sir?" the robot asked, as he hesitated and looked around.

"You're asking for answers to questions I've only begun to formulate. Come back in a few years and maybe I'll at least have the questions roughed out. But, well, it seems to me that the computers and our artificial bodies separate us. We never have to deal with each other; we always have a buffer between us. We never *touch* each other. Well, tonight I was touched by all of you." He raised the hand they'd all shaken. "And you came closer to being touched by another person than in scores of years: only one remove.''

To his surprise he saw tears on Judy's cheeks.

From the western Ahaggar, the view is out and down on the old Erg Chech, with the Tanezrouft to the south. Thatcher walked up from the adit near Ouallene with a heavy pack and a stick, pausing frequently to rest and look west. The Ahaggar was still somber, rugged, only lightly clad as yet with the verdure of the incessant storms that irrigated the land. A century was nothing to those old images.

But the Erg was now a flowery meadowland, and the foothills were forested with half a hundred kinds of trees. Life burgeoned all about him.

This area—the Hill Marches of Kabara—was sparsely settled as yet by the Game, small villages mostly of computer-animated people, pasturing sheep and cattle on the hills and scratch farming in the dales. Great fields of wheat were found only in the Plains of Shamar, below— the Erg. So scattered were the villages up here that often they had no tracks between them.

Thatcher had a three-day climb to reach his destination, the first day of it among the villages. The adit was near a town, Golthoth. The soulless ones had had word passed among them—the Thatcher was coming. Shepherd hailing shepherd passed the word among the villages that the holy hermit had come. They greeted him respectfully, offered him food and wine, and wondered to see him so young. Thatcher wondered which of them were characters. He knew that some odd souls among the human race liked the solitude and bustle of this lonely life, liked to spend years without seeing a strange face.

The second day saw him well above the villages, with only the herd-boys for company, who hallooed and yodeled to him. The third saw only the frowning, sandblasted slopes of the Ahaggar, here called the demon-haunted Mountains of Quarmall. Thatcher knew that the demons had yet to be invented.

Presently he stood upon the spot he and the computers had picked from the satellite photos, a wide bench, facing west over the Erg Chech, with the Ahaggar at its back to ward off the storms. The trees here scaled down from a century in age and a meter in diameter, and provided all manner of nuts and hardwood. There was plenty of open grassland as well, and he nodded, satisfied. From here he could not see the villages of Athne and Cathne, which lay nearest, but could see their flocks from time to time on the lower hills.

On the afternoon of his arrival, Thatcher stood looking out and down, enthralled by the dark-green/light-green view, the exhilarating shout of verdure across the land toward the setting sun. Here, he thought, a man might have leisure to deal with some really fundamental questions.

Then he turned and saw the angry gray crowd topping the Ahaggar. Hurrying, he lashed his tent with its back to the east, between big trees, taking care not to choose the tallest in the clump. Lightning was lashing the mountain behind him before he had half his wood cut; he quit chopping with but a small amount, hastily started a fire on a big rock in front of the tent, and unrolled his waterproof.

Then the storm began, and Thatcher crouched in his tiny, inadequate shelter, reflecting that he had not cut fronds to go beneath the waterproof and might spend the night in a puddle. Also, there wasn't enough wood.

He didn't get much thinking done that night. But at first light he was motivated to get out, in the freshly washed air and world, and cut wood. For this, he found his hatchet wholly inadequate, and improvised a longer handle.

I'll have to think about shelter, he thought uneasily. The prospect of building some kind of house or hut with this crude ax appalled him. Meantime, he must procure food; his small supply would not last long.

About mid-morning a herd-boy dropped in, yodeled till Thatcher answered, came over and solemnly looked at him.

"My father, 'e said, 'e says, Do you go to, Jerkin, and see 't that the Thatcher is well, 'e say," said the boy. "So, I bring you the mealie cakes my mother she make up, with butter—all but one which I eats, which she says I may be allowed." He could not hold his small body still, but his eyes were steadfast.

"Why thank you, good Jerkin, and do you convey my thanks also to your mother and father for their thought of me. It was a mighty storm, which I had scarce had time to prepare for."

"You can keep the basket—my sister Raisin makes 'em," said Jerkin, and wheeled and plunged off without further courtesy.

Thatcher's first concern was firewood and tool handles. He had the heads of a hoe and a mattock. Cutting limbs, he fitted crude handles to them. He also cut wood; it seemed this was going to be a daily chore, despite the warmth of the climate. Shelter was a concern, but it would not storm again for some days, and he could make himself comfortable in his tent.

Jerkin was followed by two more shepherds that day, bringing food and one a length of coarse grey linen cloth, used but still good. Thatcher was grateful for the interruptions; though his body was in shape, it wasn't muscled for work so strenuous as this. By the end of the day he had cut back brush and cleared the campsite. He had enough wood to hold fire overnight. He had contrived a crude hearth on a rock, moved his tent near to it, and cut fronds for his bed. He had laid out his garden plots.

Beyond that he was a little uncertain how to proceed. Even with an ax handle, his little hatchet would not suffice to build a log cabin.

The next morning Jerkin appeared as if by magic, bringing cheese and a kind word from his sister, Raisin. It reminded Thatcher that food was his next concern, if he wanted to be independent of the computers. Thatcher had brought a sling, and in his heroic career he had mastered its use. After some practice with this body, he recovered some of the old skill—it was harder without computer editing to guide his motions. He managed to bring down a squirrel and knock over a rabbit.

Back at the camp with the bodies, he found another visitor, a man of Athne.

"Maxel said, 'e said, you never goin' to build a cabin with that little hax," said the other, rising and bobbing his head nervously. "So I took thought along o' my old wife and we decided to bring ye this old cross-cut saw. That'll down them trees!''

It was old but in good condition, a meter and a half long. Thatcher thanked him profusely. ''I'll put a puncheon floor under my tent, first thing,'' he said.

''Save the bark,'' said the other. ''It be fine roofin'.''

Another man hallooed from down the hill, waved. He marched sturdily up, carrying a bulky load. ''Crombie's me name,'' he cried from a distance. ''Me wife, Pickallilli, says to me, she says, Crombie, you're not doing nothing around here—do you step up the Thatcher's hill with this bit of bakin' I've done. And so here I be!''

Thatcher was a little irked at the computers, but politely invited them to join him in his meal. Becoming exceedingly nervous, both men begged off and departed. Thatcher fried rabbit in his little spider, conscious of all his aches. And the heavy work had not yet begun.

He was happy, though. He knew he had not been this happy, in this quiet, self-satisfied way, in many decades.

He had been right to choose isolation, he thought. Among other people one is compelled to respond to their expectations. This shapes one's personality almost as completely as a Game program does, when one assumes a character's identity. For a hundred years, a hundred and fifty years, Thatcher had never been alone for long. Here, though—

''Odalayeee-ooooh!''

Thatcher jumped, nearly dropped the spider. Another visitor.

The next morning, after Jerkin's early-morning visit, Thatcher decided to postpone using the cross-cut until he had built a fish trap. This took all morning, but he mastered the craft in the process, and quickly built a couple more just before lunch, setting them in a stream that tumbled chilly out of the Ahaggar. Again a shepherd and a man of one of the villages, this time from Cathne, trudged up about noon, and again they brought food but refused to share his meal. One brought a small patched iron pot Thatcher would find useful, the other a heavy ax.

I'll not be free of their visits until the computers are convinced I can feed myself, he thought uneasily. The fish traps were a help, but he'd have to get a garden started soon. Now, though, he must hunt again—he wanted to save the food people had brought him, as it would keep.

Hunting took longer than he expected, and he came back tired with a brace of squirrels. He cut them up and put them in the pot with wild onions and new wild potatoes, set the pot to boil, and went out with the cross-cut to fell trees. By the time the stew was ready, he had cut down a tree and cut it into three three-meter lengths, one of which he had rolled to the campsite.

A shepherd stopped by on his way home, a taller, skinnier lad than Jerkin, looked curiously at the work Thatcher had done, and departed, having made sure for the computers that Thatcher was all right. The next morning he arrived with Jerkin, carrying a battered old splitting maul and three wooden wedges.

Thatcher had fish for breakfast and saw that he had enough fish in the traps to feed him fresh meat for the rest of the day. He turned one trap up so it would catch no more, and transferred the large fish from the others to it, releasing the smaller ones. Whistling over the prospect of a day with no hunting, he went to his selected spot with the mattock and starting breaking up the sod.

By the time the sun was halfway up the sky, he was ready to drop, and was ravenously hungry. He ate a bit of bread and cheese, then gave up and fried one of the fish. He needed the break, but then conscientiously went back to work, rolling the log lengths he had cut the previous day to the camp and splitting them in half. At noon, frying more fish in the spider, he brooded on the size of the plot he had broken up, and on the square area of floor he could make of his logs—about one by three meters.

This was going to take a while.

"Thatcher! Ohe! Thatcher!" It was Crombie again. This time he bore dried meat and an old but not decrepit bucksaw. "This'll save your back, your reverence!" he cried. "No need to chop your firewood to length no more! You should make a sawbuck, though. You know—a sawhorse."

Again Thatcher tried to pay, and again money was waved away.

Crombie was the only visitor that noon, and Thatcher flung himself grimly into his work, determined to show the computers he needed no help. He laid his puncheon floor, re-pitched his tent, cut and split firewood, overhauled his hearth. In the cool of the evening he again took mattock in hand for the hardest work of his new life.

He had had time to think, however, and instead of trying to break up a square plot, he dug a long narrow strip. Poached fish for supper, and then he collapsed into bed.

Jerkin awoke him very early, and he dragged himself groaning out in the chill dewy predawn. He was not awake enough to be hungry, contenting himself with a mealie cake Jerkin had brought.

"You can keep that clay pot," said Jerkin, going from foot to foot. "My sister Raisin, she made it special for you."

Thatcher dug viciously at the sod with his mattock while it was still cool, and after a couple of hours, sweating freely, he had doubled the width of his long row. Taking time to fry eggs and fish, he planted beans along it. It would never do to wait planting on the whole garden; it might take him a month at this rate.

Fortunately the Sahara had two growing seasons and no real winter.

The rest of the day Thatcher grimly cut down trees and limbed them. The noon visitors, bringing this time clay pots, reed baskets, and soap, cheerfully helped him get them to the campsite. Thatcher had decided to build a cabin five meters square, so he was cutting trees about twice that tall at maximum; the tops he could use for many things, if only firewood. He wanted fairly small logs, as he didn't know how much help he would have in piling them up.

Next morning, Jerkin brought a kitten from Raisin, which Thatcher dubbed Mischa. She was a suspicious-eyed creature, quite small but very self-possessed, who investigated the camp disdainfully then disappeared. Thatcher had fed her a piece of fish, and wasn't worried.

* * *

A few days later Crombie arrived, panting under a load of wheat. Thatcher had solved the problem of their generosity by buying wheat; a shilling bought so much it took several trips for Crombie to tote it up. With him were other visitors, this time from farther away than Athne or Cathne.

"Master," said one, when Thatcher approached, his ax over his shoulder. "We have come—"

Shrill uproar. Startled, they all looked about. "A cat!" Crombie cried.

"Mischa!" Thatcher ran for the stream, followed by his visitors.

The little cat was in the upright trap in which Thatcher stored his captured fish. She squalled and flailed about frantically, splashing and scaring the fish. Thatcher started to reach for her, checked.

"Don't 'ee do it, Master!" cried Crombie. "She'll chaw ye to—"

But he *couldn't* leave her while he found a stick. With a quick snatch he got her by the neck and lifted her. In a flash Mischa had her claws in his hand, turning bonelessly about. Thatcher gasped and nearly fell into the stream, threw himself backward. Mischa only let go when he thumped her, hand and all, onto the ground. Then she vanished, swearing.

Stunned, Thatcher sat on the muddy bank, dripping blood, and looked at his equally dumbfounded guests. After a moment he plunged his hand into the icy stream.

"Uh—Master," said the spokesman of the visitors,

weakly. "We, uh, we h-have come to ask of you the riddle of Life."

The cold water numbed the pain. Thatcher took his hand out of the stream, looked at it blankly, and to gain time, said, "Let us make ourselves comfortable."

The riddle of Life? Back at the campsite he invited them to join him in his meal, and as they had brought food, they agreed to do so. They ate, chatting inconsequentially, though the visitors were nervous in the presence of the Great Man. Crombie also stayed, bobbing his head much and saying little, visibly agog to learn the answer to their question.

Thatcher had spent his life avoiding Life. He had come here to find, in a way, the answer to that riddle. Still . . . latent in his decision to leave the Game was a provisional answer, he found. And at meal's end, he told them solemnly:

"Life is a riddle solved by living."

When they had gone, awestruck and thankful for this revelation, he nursed his slashed hand and wondered if that statement had any meaning. He suspected it was circular. In any case, one would have to do quite a bit of living to know if it was true or not. As he was doing now, he supposed. Thatcher stretched, feeling the protest of his muscles, still not inured to this life. He was covered with bruises acquired in cutting and rolling logs, his hands had had the bark knocked off so often they were a mass of scabs, his knees were sore from frequent kneeling over various tasks, and despite the altitude and the ceaseless light wind, it was hot.

That's living, he told himself. The Game was certainly never like this.

In that, he concluded next day that he was mistaken.

Near noon, trailing his hoe tiredly, he strolled to the edge of the bench and looked wearily down, almost too exhausted to begin cooking—too tired even to feel very hungry. And saw, approaching, a colorfully-garbed cluster of visitors who had to be from Golthoth, the small town at the foot of the slopes. More pilgrims seeking answers.

And he, he had not had a moment in which to think.

Thatcher remembered Taratan's conviction that the Gods played at Life and Death with Mankind to keep it from learning the secrets of existence. He flung up his fist against the Ahaggar and cried, "*You sons of bitches!*"

11

If I Only Had a Brain

As the high Saharan summer wore on, Thatcher worked. He dug with his mattock two hours a day, morning and evening, in the coolth. He planted and hoed in the mattocked soil. He sawed down trees, sawed them up, split them, rolled them to the site of his cabin. He dug and toted rocks till his sturdy muscles ached, and laid them up into a hearth and chimney.

All this he did between interruptions, though to do them credit his visitors willingly helped—most of them—at whatever task he was engaged in. He was less helpful to them.

They came to ask him of affairs in Shamar. They came to ask if he sought an apprentice to learn his Mystery. They came to ask if he could pierce the Veil and restore to them the words of their beloveds. They came to ask if he could locate lost valuables. They came to ask him to foretell their futures.

But Thatcher had learned his lesson, and steadfastly refused to answer any of the queries.

A party of villagers, laughing, then sobering in his revered presence, climbed the hill to pile his cut and notched logs into a cabin. Thatcher blessed them in the name of some Game god he'd never previously heard of.

Bit by bit he mattocked and planted his garden, laid in a puncheon floor in the cabin, cobbled together a crude table and a corded bedstead, a few shelves on the wall. He dug a root cellar in a bank, lined it with stone.

He bought a few simple articles of ironmongery to cook in, in addition to his old spider, but cooking he found to be a perennial nuisance. Bread in particular gave him trouble. When he acquired his super trit wheat, he toasted it and ground it on a crude metate contrived on a flat rock, achieving a coarse meal.

He finally got a sourdough start going, using mashed acorn milk, and with that as a beginning was ready to attempt sourdough bread. But the whole-grain flour was brown and nutlike in flavor and texture, the resulting bread too hard to eat.

His constant refusal to respond chilled the ardor of his pilgrims, and the computers overrode their Game programming. The stream of company dwindled to a few helpful villagers as he began to achieve self-sufficiency. Finally only Jerkin was left, still, dropping in every second or third morning.

But acquiring foodstuffs did not give him food.

Thatcher tried again for bread, mixing butter and salt

and hot water (no milk available) and a plentiful supply of the sourdough starter with the heavy dark flour. He stirred it up with a big wooden spoon in a tight basket. Then he wallowed this dough out onto a stump, kneading it and adding flour, till it was of the right consistency. Next: let it rise in the sun, covered against flies. When it had doubled in bulk in the basket, he punched it down, let it rise again to double bulk. Punch down, cut into loaves, and again double in bulk—the whole process took nearly half a day before the baking began.

Again he overbaked, nor was his hearth easy to regulate.

Jerkin began to talk up a visit by his sister Raisin, who was interested in the holy hermit. So the computers, Thatcher thought, irked but amused, were determined to see that he lacked no comfort. He seriously considered permitting the visit, if only for her advice on his cooking. Bread wasn't his only failure; bland soups and stews and tough-frying were the only ways he had of cooking his meat. Roasts were beyond his skill with his primitive means.

He could and did make porridge out of his meal, and a shingle-like hoecake. But lightbread escaped him. Finally he mentioned his perplexity to Jerkin, who, after a day or two, remembered to bring up some of ''Raisin's good yeast.''

The yeast bread turned out like the sourdough, and he inquired of Jerkin specifically Raisin's method of baking. Raisin, all too happy to help, sent up her mother's dutch ovens, and at last he acquired a tolerable bread. Still too hard and tough for any but his new teeth. It had taken him three weeks. He considered it a triumph.

The garden too was a triumph. He had known a garden when he was a boy—the fascination had escaped him then. Now he found it absorbing. There was an undercurrent of sadness in his happiness. Taratan would have loved this, he thought, and wondered if he had caught the gardening bug from the big man. Wiping his eyes and laughing as he picked tomatoes, Thatcher recalled Taratan's blood-ruby. He supposed it really had been a ruby, a synthetic one. Not all the gems in the Game were real, some were merely glass. How could the characters tell? This, however, was the true treasure.

"Better than twenty-three cents and ten free beers, anyway," he said.

When at last Thatcher could no longer postpone the visit of the ministering angel, Raisin shyly accompanied Jerkin one midday. A mousy blonde girl, on the border of womanhood, slightly plump, attractive in an earthy way. Computer-animated, of course, shyly but eagerly interested in the holy hermit. He supposed it was permissible for her to sleep with his holy self; sex was as freely available in the Game as outside, or more so.

Though Thatcher found her more appealing than any of his visitors save Jerkin, he was relieved to find her so shy. She was barely able to discuss cooking with him. The meeting ended with vague promises of future ones, and Thatcher hoped the computers behind her would realize he was not seeking companionship.

Thatcher's labors did not ease with the building of his cabin and the digging of his garden, as he had expected. The garden required constant work, and the cabin was always in some way inadequate.

From being a holy hermit sitting on a rock, he had become quite a wealthy man, cumbered about with cares and things to care for. Thatcher smiled at that, but had no leisure to pursue it. His fireplace smoked.

To work effectively, a fireplace must have a smoke shelf, or step—the Tory American, later Count Rumford, first pointed this out. Thatcher finally remembered the proper construction of fireplaces from something that had come up in the Game forty years before. Tired of having his head smoked off, he let the fire die and peered into the fireplace, and nodded.

First he'd have to disassemble the fireplace proper to get at the back wall of the chimney, along which he must lay a new course of rocks. Accordingly he began to tug rocks out and lay them aside. Perhaps he should number them ''for just such an emergency,'' he thought.

Then the chimney gave out the deep-toned sound of stone on stone, as if the earth should clear her throat, and disintegrated. Thatcher flung himself back but was borne farther back into the cabin and half buried. He hit his head a sickening crack on the puncheon floor, felt consciousness fade. Dimly he realized that this felt about the same as if in a Game body.

He awoke to the pain in his right leg.

Sitting up with an effort, feeling weak and dizzy, Thatcher looked at his legs. They were half buried in a rock pile, and were bruised and battered. The right knee felt particularly bad. But below the knee was where the pain concentrated: under that big ugly rock. Giving way to panic, Thatcher braced his palms on the log floor and pushed, trying to pull himself out of the rocks. A yell of

pain from his legs notified him of his error; now he had
pulled muscles all up and down them.

He sat panting, calming himself. He'd have to lift
them off. Reaching awkwardly, he gradually cleared the
rocks away, all but the big one. He had to rest before
tackling that one, and again after, when he thought he
might scream with the pain. This wasn't a bit like being
in a Game body. Finally, gasping on a high note, he ran
his finger down the line of the bone below the knee.

Pain!

He thought—*pain*—the bone wasn't—*pain*—displaced,
merely a fracture—*pain*. It wasn't going——*pain*—going
to be necessary—*pain pain pain*—to set his leg—*pain*.
Thatcher gently pulled the swollen leg up—*pain, pain,
pain* in the knee—and considered. He could probably
even get to his foot, hobble around with a stick. There
was enough food on hand to see him through. Jerkin was
coming by every two or three days.

Merely a hairline fracture of the tibia. Or was it the
fibula? He thought, if he could get to the bed, he'd be all
right. Thatcher considered that and a hint of anxiety
entered his thoughts. It wasn't serious; he should be able
to hobble around, and in a couple of days should be fairly
ambulatory.

He was feverish and ill. Water might be more critical
than food. And he was all alone here. If he slipped and
fell—

Thatcher felt very tired. He lay back on the floor,
carefully, carefully, and turned his head aside. Out through
the door he could see one of the patches of his garden. It

looked very peaceful and far away. The shadows had grown; he must have been out for a couple of hours.

Turning his head the other way, he saw the shovel Jerkin's pa had loaned him. It would have to do. Inching his way toward it, dragging his protesting leg after him, he crossed the floor, accumulating splinters.

Knocking the shovel down on himself, he braced it upside down and gradually pulled himself up into a standing position on his bruised and quivering left leg. The right leg, with its battered knee, could take no weight, even discounting the break. He decided—head swimming with pain—that he needed rest most of all. The shovel made a very inadequate crutch, but he shuffled to the bed in the far corner. Have to make a better crutch tomorrow.

No sooner had he stretched himself out on the bed than he felt the outraged muscles of both legs begin to scream. Spasms rippled along his legs; the muscles seemed to flutter like flags in a wind. Withal, his right foot was partially numb, and he suspected he might never fully recover use of it. It was obvious that he wasn't getting up from here soon—and the next stress on those muscles would produce a reaction as severe.

Why, he could actually die here before the computers knew.

With a sudden clarity, looking toward the door where he could still see a corner of his garden, Thatcher thought, I've been a fool.

All this work—the garden, what a triumph, the house, independence, my own body—all worth nothing more than a shekel a day! I might as well have stayed in the

Game for all I've done with myself. He writhed with a deeper pain than the physical. What had he said? He'd have leisure to consider fundamental problems!

Quotidian, he thought, trying to soothe his angry leg muscles, his face in a permanent grimace of pain. The day-to-day details of living had overwhelmed him. "Life is a riddle whose solution is Living," indeed. Had he thought he was living, just because he'd cast off the Game body?

Thatcher writhed again with self-contempt. Taratan would have been disappointed in him.

Should have gone straight to Australia, he thought. Quotidian there too, but I could've done something. The computers practically begged me to help. Tried to duck out again. Hard to break a lifetime's habit of avoiding problems.

Then came the thunder, and the storm. Darkness and rain, and then the night. The chill soothed the pain in his legs but stiffened his muscles, nor did it ease his thirsty feverishness.

He awoke to the cat's yowl. Mischa stood on his chest, glaring at him, eyes huge in the pale light of predawn. But Thatcher could not bring himself to move. Eventually she bounced resentfully away. When full light returned it found him tossing uneasily on the bed, trying to nerve himself for the effort of rising. He must have water. He felt he would die without water.

Then he saw the small person standing in the doorway, peering in at him: definitely not Jerkin. Hooded, shadowed, and sinister.

Life, thought Thatcher inconsequentially, is a riddle solved by Death.

"Aye," said a voice from the door.

Thatcher blinked and looked again. Indeed there was a child-sized someone there, wearing dark gray and light gray, curiously hard to see, despite the bright eyes under the hood. This person entered slowly, gaze fixed on Thatcher. Behind him loomed another shadow, a huge one, dressed in linen and leathers and studded with brass, with a sword hilt protruding over the shoulder. The smaller man, Thatcher saw, wore a curved rapier and a knife, and carried a horn-handled sling.

"Hola!" cried the small man gaily, glancing about one last time for hidden enemies. "You'd be the Thatcher, not so?" With a humorous quirk of his mobile features up through the nonexistent ceiling to the bark roof.

This fellow was swarthy, olive-skinned, and cultured; every mannerism bespoke some great metropolitan center. The huge man was obviously a barbarian, copper-haired, with clear sea-green eyes. He was as tall as Taratan and nearly as big, and seemed to move slowly. Thatcher was not fooled; those mighty muscles could burst into murderous motion in a moment.

Heroes, hell-bent for their shekel a day.

"A bit of an accident?" The little man looked at the pile of rocks covering the floor, the hole in the wall where the fireplace and chimney had stood.

"Fractured leg," Thatcher said wearily. "I'll probably be all right in a few days, or at least able to hobble around. You don't die of a broken leg."

"Unless you have infection. Let's have a look. Fetch water, Farfar."

The heroes turned to and made him comfortable, the giant barbarian carrying him as tenderly as a baby to the outhouse, and they made him a crutch. Thatcher knew, of course, that the moment these characters set eyes on him the computers had gone into alarm. At this very moment, no doubt, Jerkin was hurrying his sheep to their pasture before answering a strong impulse to come over and see to the Thatcher. Perhaps someone else in Athne had a sudden urge to go and speak to the holy man.

"Will you be all right?" the little man asked, when they had packed his legs with cold compresses and put out food for Mischa.

"Quite well, thank you. Friends will be by before noon, and I should do well enough till then."

"Best we go, then," said the big man. "We want no witnesses."

"We trust you'll tell no one we came by," said the little man wryly, and Thatcher nodded. "We seek to cross the Quarmalls, which have an evil reputation. Can you tell us of the demons there?"

"They do not yet exist," Thatcher said incautiously. Too late he remembered that the little man, Gray Malkin, had studied magic in his youth. The players of these characters were a pair of lesbian lovers with a strong sense of humor.

"Do not yet exist," said the little man, musingly. "Tell me, holy man, what is the secret of life? You mentioned it—"

Thatcher pulled himself up sitting, despite the pain,

feeling his face congested with rage. "Fuck off!" he shouted.

Farfar bellowed with laughter. The little man grimaced up at him: "Yak it up, Grandfather!"

"Sic him, Catkin!" cried the big man. "Strangle him! Tear his tongue out!"

Their humor—even Gray Malkin was smiling wryly and apologetic—recalled Thatcher. "Sorry," he said. "I was just berating myself for having avoided that question, before you came."

"Some say that the world is illusion, that it does not truly exist," said the little man, still obviously revolving the demons that did not yet exist. He looked questioningly at Thatcher.

Thatcher sighed, eased his cramped legs. "It is less real than it seems to you, but it is very real," he said. "And quite ridiculous."